RAPTURE

C.N. CRAWFORD

To discuss this and other books, please join my facebook group, C.N. Crawford's Coven.
In order to stay up to date with book releases, you can check out my website to sign up to my newsletter: www.cncrawford.com

I

NIGHT OF THE HARROWING

Glass had sliced through my skin. Under the night sky, I plummeted through the air. Time stretched out, and I dropped in slow motion. Blood streamed from the cuts, from the gash in my side.

We were supposed to be married tomorrow, but she was gone now. This was what it meant to fall: it meant losing your reason for existing.

The drop seemed eternal, all sense of fear dulled under cotton wool. My engagement ring glinted in the night, a little sliver of sunlight in the darkness.

As I fell closer to the moat, the certainty of death pierced me like a blade. This was the end of everything. Panic bloomed in my mind—the fear of things unfinished and questions unanswered.

At last, I slammed down hard into the murky moat, my back arching with the pain, bones breaking with the force of the fall. Sharp cracks shot through my legs, my spine. Agony sank into my brain like thorns, robbing me of coherent thought. I thought I needed to swim to the surface, but my body was too broken to move properly. In the dark, I didn't know up from down.

Sinking, I drifted under the gloom. Dark water enveloped me, claiming me.

A flash of gold gleamed in the dark. Under the surface of the water, my ring glinted—a bright spark in the murk. I wanted to pull the cursed thing off, but that was a waste of energy.

This had happened before. This had *all* happened before.

Streaks of crimson mingled with the dark water.

I was still alive, and that meant I could still find a way out of this. Just as soon as I could figure out up from down, as soon as I could command my broken limbs to move again.

Air. Air.

My lungs were ready to explode. I couldn't breathe, and my throat was starting to spasm. Desperate, I tried to kick my shattered legs.

Could I drag myself, fingers clawing in the dirt, from the moat before I drowned? No matter what had happened in the past, I'd always found a way out.

At last, I realized silver rays of light were piercing the surface. That way was up. I could make it if I blocked out the pain in my body. Shockingly, I was still alive.

But as I swam higher, dread unfurled in my chest. From under the water, I caught a glimpse of pale blond hair over a black shirt. Alice stood above me, flanked by a line of the Free Men.

How had she managed to get here?

As soon as I came up for air, they'd drag me out. A world of pain awaited me.

2

LILA
THREE WEEKS EARLIER

Sighing, I stared down at the curving moat far below, its surface dark and murky. Beneath the window of my luxurious prison suite in the Iron Fortress, three stories of sleek black rock gleamed in the moonlight. There was no way I could climb out of here—no crevices to stick my fingers into, no footholds to help me escape. I'd been trapped here for months.

Months ago, I'd been locked up in Castle Saklas, on a cliff off the coast of Albia. That lasted about five days. Then, in the middle of the night, four guards had dragged me out to a boat. They kept cloaks up, hiding their faces. No one spoke to me as we travelled down the Dark River to Dovren, but I wondered if I was going to be executed. Instead, they brought me back to the city and locked me in the Iron Fortress--a place I'd seen from afar, but never wanted to enter.

But I was brewing a plan.

I pressed my hands against the cold glass, yearning for the moment I would roam free again, even if it looked bleak as hell out there. Winter had spread its frosty mantle over the world, and a light dusting of snow and ice coated everything. Beyond the moat, a thorny, untended garden rambled over the grounds, stretching out to an iron gate. Tall and gothic, it was known as the Iron Fortress because of the formidable spiked fence around it. Maybe I'd be out there soon.

It was a different sort of fortress these days. The iron fence lay half in ruins, but angelic magic protected this place from intruders. No one could get in unless someone from the inside allowed them in.

And as for getting out? I was working on that.

I'd been staring out this window far too long, in the same nightgown I'd been wearing for months. No one had given me a change of clothes, not even when I'd moved locations. In the past few months, I'd memorized every curve of the serpentine river just beyond the gate. Tonight, a heavy fog rolled off the water, pierced by warm lights from gas lamps. I could just about make out two figures walking along the bank.

An ache pierced my chest. Maybe I could be with another person soon ...

How amazing that would be. It had been at least two months since I'd seen another person.

At least, I *thought* I'd been in here two months. It could just as well have been eleven years. It was hard to track time when loneliness clouded my thoughts like a sickness, making it hard to breathe. Every day, my meals arrived in a little dumbwaiter with a wooden door. It wasn't large enough for me to fit in, though I'd definitely tried.

Before I'd been locked in here, Samael's beautiful face had been the last I'd seen. Since then, I thought he might have forgotten I existed. Once, I'd caught a glimpse of him brooding by the River Walk, his cloak drawn up over his head. I stuck my head out the window, shouting and trying to get his attention. I longed for just a glimpse of those pale gray eyes, but it was like he couldn't hear me at all. I desperately wanted him to look at me. No such luck.

But I supposed there were worse things than loneliness. I had, after all, tried to murder him with a bomb. In response, he'd locked me in a luxurious room stacked with books. I'd spent the time practicing reading on my own, sounding out words. Memorizing sounds and letters.

Another silver lining of my prison: it wasn't anything like the dungeons of Castle Hades, where traitors had been tortured for thousands of years. I hadn't lost skin, nor fingernails, nor eyeballs. Both my ears remained attached to my head, and not a single burning rod had been inserted into any of my orifices. I had no broken bones. I hadn't been dipped in a vat of boiling oil, not even once.

And that was frankly bloody lucky, because Samael was the closest thing we had to a king, and I'd nearly murdered him. Regicides didn't normally get a soft bed and three meals a day. They normally had their entrails ripped out before their eyes.

I should count my lucky stars in here.

There were, however, two teensy weensy problems with my current situation, which was why I was working on breaking out.

One, I had some vengeance to wreak, and my imprisonment was getting in my way. My former friend and my sister had brutally betrayed me, putting my life at risk. They were the reason I was locked up here.

And two, I was losing my ever-loving mind in isolation. There was no torture rack or Catherine wheel, but there was endless solitude. The closest thing I had to contact with another person was when I heard the squeaking of the dumbwaiter and knew someone was pulling it from the kitchens below. Three times a day, a delicious meal of meat and vegetables and a sinfully sweet red fruit with seeds that made my mouth water appeared—arranged on the tray by another person.

I was better fed than ever, but I'd never been alone before. I'd even shared a bed with my mum, since we just had the one.

At times, I was sure a phantom presence was watching me. A malign spirit seemed to linger in the shadows, waiting. Once, I'd even thought I'd seen a woman out of the corner of my eyes. Her dark hair waved around her head like she was underwater, her arms raised, wrists limp.

But mostly, I thought I was going mad.

The hair on the back of my neck rose, and I shuddered as I stared out the window. It was that feeling again, of being watched. It was almost like someone knew I wanted to escape.

Slowly, I turned, narrowing my eyes to survey the room. In the dead of night, moonlight spilled over the bookshelves, the wooden dresser. The wick on the lantern was nearly burned down, growing dim. For a moment, the shadows seemed to be shifting, darkness flitting from one corner to another.

But when I scanned the room more carefully, I saw everything as it should be: a four-poster bed; the stark silver and black banners hanging on either side, with the Angelic writing I couldn't read. The mirror hung over the dresser, by the locked door. The bathroom door was shut, as I'd left it. Nothing amiss.

Just my lonely mind playing tricks on me again. I exhaled slowly.

Facing the window again, I turned the crank to open it a little bit. The wind howled inside, the cold sharpening my senses. *Keep your wits about you, Lila.*

I stuck my head out the open window and clutched the windowsill. It was just about wide enough to get my head out, so I'd been shoving my face into frigid air a *lot*. I needed to cool down. At night, dreams of Samael tormented me, and I'd wake up feverish and overheated. I kept dreaming of him tying my hands above my head. While I was tied up, he slowly stripped off my clothes, torturing me with a light touch that made me gasp. He'd brush his mouth over my body, his breath warming me and making me insane with desire. He'd stroke me and tease me, but never satiate me.

Then I'd wake up again, my body on fire. Unsatisfied. I'd rush over to the window and stick my head into the icy wind.

I was coming to realize that angels were addictive that way. Samael was a forbidden fruit I never should have tasted. I'd had one night with him, one taste, and now I'd never forget the feel of his lips against mine. No mortal man would ever satisfy me.

I'd given up thinking I could change his mind. In here, I'd been completely forgotten, with no chance to speak to him. And maybe once I escaped, I could forget him a little better.

I just needed the raven to show up.

"Jenny Squawks!" I whispered into the wind. "You are my only friend."

Absolute lunatic. I'd given the raven a name, and she was a central part of my escape plan. It had taken a few weeks of practice, but I'd trained her to bring me things. I would show her something metallic, and coax her to bring me *other* little shiny things: pennies, a little spoon, a butter knife that she tried to drag across the room. Specifically, I was hoping she'd find long, thin bits of metal. Something I could use as a lockpick.

When she completed her tasks, I always gave her a bite of the delicious red fruit.

Eventually, she would come back with a shiny thing I could use. At least, I hoped. So far, I had a collection of coins, a screw, two spoons, and a broken monocle.

As I searched for her in the night, the wind bit at my skin. I moved back into the room, sitting down on the bed.

This had been the only plan I could come up with.

"Lila."

An unfamiliar, rasping voice spoke from behind me, making my heart pound harder. I gripped the windowsill hard.

I wasn't alone here after all.

3

LILA

With a racing pulse, I turned around. A strange voice had just rasped my name, and yet I couldn't see anyone in here.

My heart hammered my ribs. The shadows seemed to twist and writhe over the room like smoke. A chill washed over me.

"I know you're there," I whispered. "Whoever you are. Whatever you are. But whatever you're doing, it's just not on. I'm not having it." The most useless threat in the history of threats, perhaps, but I was doing my best.

Swallowing hard, I took another step to investigate. But as I walked past the mirror, something turned my blood to ice. From the corner of my eye, I saw a shadow behind me.

One millimeter at a time, I turned my head, hardly daring to look. And when I had a full view of the reflection, I froze.

There, behind me in the reflection, stood the silhouette of a woman. Wild hair snaked around her head, in front of her face. Her arms were raised in the air, wrists limp, like she was floating under water.

She was a nightmare come to life.

I froze in place, staring at her. Was I losing my mind?

As I gaped at the reflection behind me, I felt water rising up my throat, my esophagus. Rotten water was filling my lungs, coming out of my mouth.

Panic screamed in my mind, and I fell to my knees hard. Wet leaves filled my mouth. I was choking, suffocating. Flailing, I tried to call out, but my screams were trapped under the sodden leaves in my throat. I reached in, pulling out the muck, but it just filled again, like the earth itself was choking me.

My lungs were going to explode. I was going to die here, completely alone. Was this Samael's magic? Was this punishment for what I'd done? My thoughts were starting to go black.

Then, the illusion simply disappeared. Clutching my throat, I gasped, breathing in as deep as I could. I fell back on the floor, my limbs bruised.

I took a deep breath, in and out, filling my lungs.

At last, the pain was gone. Tears streamed down my face, my whole body shaking. I swiped my hand over my mouth, still trying to rid it of phantom leaves. But they were just gone, completely.

"What is going on?" I whispered.

For good luck, I touched the little raven tattoo on my bicep. *Blessed Raven King, give me strength.* Already, I felt myself relaxing.

Slowly, I stood on shaking legs. Swallowing hard, I turned to the mirror again—and I found the silhouette behind me.

I whirled this time, ready to attack.

But there was no one, nothing behind me. Just the bed, the moonlight, and the empty room.

"What the hell?" I shouted. "I am warning you ... I will really make you upset if you don't stop this!"

Wonderful. I'd come up with an even *more* useless threat.

But I was being attacked by a ghost, it seemed. How did you threaten something that was already dead?

I breathed in and out slowly, trying to marshal a sense of calm. Maybe I was going completely barmy. I glanced back in the mirror, relieved to see the apparition was gone.

A fluttering of wings turned my head, and relief unclenched my chest as my raven friend swooped into the room. Even better, she carried something shiny and metallic in her beak. When she dropped it on the floor, it clanged against the stone.

Sighing, I rushed forward. "You genius, Jenny Squawks."

When I picked her treasure up, I saw it was much more expensive than I'd been expecting. Jenny had brought me a hair clip shaped like a leaf, inset with diamonds. It looked antique and worth a fortune. "This is beautiful, Jenny."

But the real question was, why did Samael have something like this? How many rich women lived in this castle?

Did he have a lover?

Nothing to do with me if he did, really. We were not speaking. I turned the clip over and examined the thin metal clasp on the back. It was long, and bendable enough that I could actually use it to pick the lock.

I just needed another one like it.

I looked up at Jenny, who had cocked her head, waiting for her reward. I reached out to pet her head, and she flapped her wings, squawking loudly.

"Good job," I said. "You've done very good work here, Jenny. Brilliant."

But it wasn't praise she wanted. I crossed to my leftover fruit—fruit pieces that looked like little red glittering beads. I dropped a few pieces before her, and she gobbled them down, then cocked her head again, looking at me expectantly.

"Don't you worry, little bird. I have another task for you. I need a second hair clip." I pointed at it, then pointed at the window, and Jenny was off again, swooping outside.

While I waited for her, I turned the bejeweled hair clip over in my hand once more. The craftsmanship was exquisite. The diamonds had to be worth tens of thousands of crowns. Was this a relic of the Albian royals who'd once lived here?

Touching my throat again, I scanned the room for signs of the ghost. My gaze flicked above, where the ceiling rose to sharp peaks—dark stone carved with intricate, thorny engravings. Everything looked normal.

I glanced in the mirror again, my body rigid with fear.

The rumors in Dovren were that this Iron Fortress had been built five hundred years ago. A king had kept his beautiful mistress somewhere in the castle. Her name had been lost to history, so everyone called her the Iron Queen. Once Alice had tried to draw a picture of her—with long legs and pale skin, black hair, and a crown of long thorns. Legend held that the king had loved her so much he'd locked her up in one of these rooms so she could never leave. She'd died in here.

Some said she'd gone mad in captivity, feral. To be honest, right now, I was relating to her a little too much. And what if *this* had been her room?

When Jenny came flying back through the window again, another bejeweled hair clip clutched in her talons, my chest unclenched. *Nearly to freedom.*

"Jenny, you absolute beauty."

Finally, I would be free. I could find Zahra, and hug another human again before I figured out my next move. Then, I supposed I'd have to live in disguise so Samael never found me again. Ernald would never take me back after the bomb incident.

But even the ragged paupers had something to do with their days, a way to earn a penny. After all, *someone* had to clean the streets of horse manure.

I knelt before the door. With shaking hands, I got to work as quickly as I could, sliding the long hair pins into the lock. I felt around a little, trying to work out the shape of the lock. It was a complex mechanism, but with years of experience, I was able to gently compress one pin after another, moving my way through.

Perhaps Samael had scoured the room for lockpick items, but it seemed he hadn't anticipated that I would train a raven.

"Lila!" It was the ghost's gargling voice behind me, making my heart slam. *"Where do you think you're going? This is your home. Don't you want to know how you'll die here?"*

"Absolutely not." I was trying to work faster now, rushing.

At last, I compressed the final pin. When I heard the lock click open, my heart leapt with relief.

I was going to break out of my prison at last, and I would never see these four walls again.

4
SAMAEL

I gripped the stone arches above me, trying to focus on the simple movement of pulling myself up, then lowering myself down again. It was a pointless exercise, but I liked the burn in my muscles. In the ruined church, I'd been moving my body up and down again for ... I didn't know how long. Hours? My arms burned, but I was losing myself in the pleasure of the ache.

I breathed in the scent of life around me—the moss growing on the crumbling stone, the grasses carpeting the ground. Silvered rays of moonlight streamed through the fog, illuminating the sharp peaks of a half-ruined medieval church. The ceiling had crumbled long ago, and now a misty sky hung above me. From here, I could see one of the towers of the Iron Fortress stretching up into the clouds.

Lately, my senses were sharpened, sometimes overwhelmingly so. The rich tastes of food delighted me; the feel of alcohol burning my throat made me feel alive.

Something had changed in me since my brush with death. Since Lila had tried to murder me.

There was a destructive side to me, one I'd kept under the surface since the early days of the fall. Sourial called it my reaper side—the one that slaughtered with abandon. I could hardly remember it, but Sourial claimed that, when I'd first fallen, I'd left piles of the dead in my wake. The reaper enjoyed the kill. The reaper didn't understand love or mercy. That side of me had once watched Yvonne burn to death and failed to step in.

Now, I was a hair's breadth away from losing my mind, ready to plunge into the abyss of madness at any moment. Hell of a time for me to become King of the Fallen.

And yet, I felt stronger than ever.

I wanted to rule.

I hoisted myself up again, reveling in the power coursing through my body. I hadn't felt so far from Heaven in ages. But maybe I liked it a little. Once more, I pulled myself up, my fingers gripping the stonework above the arch. Then, I lowered my body down again.

The sound of footfalls made me pause, and I let myself drop to the ground. In the billowing fog, my fingers twitched at the hilt of my sword.

It was only when I saw Sourial's blue cloak through the mist that I started to relax.

He crossed through the archway and leaned against one of the ruined walls, folding his arms. "Where were you?"

"What do you mean? I was here." I said it like it was normal to lurk in a dark, ruined church all night.

"The Fallen Council met, as planned," he replied. "You were supposed to be there. We were discussing the conditions for you to become king."

I stared at him. How had I forgotten? "Oh, that," I said quietly. Confusion slid through my mind. I had no idea what day it was anymore. "Do you have any whiskey?"

Sourial fell silent for a moment. "Since when do you drink alcohol?"

I flashed him a smile. "Since I nearly died and started learning to enjoy the world around me."

He pulled out his little silver flask and arched a quizzical eyebrow. "I notice that you're lurking outside the castle where you've imprisoned Lila. Is she on your mind, by any chance?"

I took a sip and let the smoky whiskey roll over my tongue. Why had I gone so long without this? "No. I haven't been thinking about Lila at all. What are the conditions, then, for me to rule as king?"

"Before they will crown you, you must swear an oath to kill the Harrower. I don't suppose you know where you'd find the Harrower?"

My muscles tightened. "The Free Men haven't yet summoned the demon."

"How do you know?"

"I'll feel it as soon as they do. I'm working on finding out as much as I can. What else?"

"You must follow the custom of the Fallen—take at least one mortal wife."

I leaned back against the wall, considering this. They had given me clear directives. Unfortunately, I hadn't the faintest clue where the Free Men were anymore, let alone how close they were to raising the Harrower. The effort of trying to stay sane had been consuming my thoughts completely. I needed to focus better.

I scrubbed my hand over my jaw. "So I must marry Lila."

He snatched the whiskey from me. "No, you must marry a mortal. Not Lila. She tried to murder us both with a *bomb*. I may not be an expert in matters of the heart, but I'd say that makes her a bad choice for a wife."

How could I explain this to him? "I've always been guided

by my dreams. They've always kept me on the right path, kept me from descending into madness. And my dreams tell me she will help me find the Harrower. When I sleep, I see Lila wearing a wedding gown, leading me on a path to the Harrower. So, this is what I must do."

Sourial took a step closer, his eyes shining in the moonlight. His gaze was too sharp, too keen. "But it's not working now, is it? Your reaper side is coming back."

I cocked my head. "I'm fine."

"You don't remember the massacres I witnessed in the old days, Samael. Your dreams of ruling as king will lie in ruins if you lose your mind. You'll be worse than the Free Men."

"Maybe my reaper side is only surfacing because I haven't yet married Lila. It is my destiny, even if it's all for show."

He went very still, shadows thickening around him. "She nearly murdered us both. What if she escapes again and passes information on to the Free Men? Or gets another bomb?"

"She won't be able to. She will remain locked in the castle. We'll just have a public wedding. She'll help me find the Harrower. I'll kill the demon, become king, and lock her in her room again when the ceremony is over. I will forget she exists."

In theory.

"Are you sure she's actually mortal?" said Sourial. "Could she be a demon? Or nephilim? We both know she used magic."

I shuddered at the word *demon*. "She's not a demon. Have you ever seen a demon without black eyes? Nephilim, perhaps, but she doesn't smell like a nephilim. She's mortal. Some angel must have taught her magic. It's the only explanation." An inexplicable jolt of jealousy shot through me at the thought, and my jaw tightened.

Sourial narrowed his eyes. "And how are you so sure she won't escape?"

I walked past him. "I can promise you that if she tries to escape this time, she will regret it deeply. Her freedom won't last long."

5

LILA

As I crept barefoot through the dark halls, I felt as if the ghost stalked behind me, breathing down my neck. The air in the castle was frigid; I hugged myself. Since I'd woken up in that room, wearing nothing but a thin white nightgown, no one had brought me clothes.

When I got out into the world, I'd be running through Dovren's streets half naked and freezing. My bare feet would turn to ice on the cobbles. Still, it was better than taking my chances with the ghost.

Shivering, I turned a corner in the dark corridor. Shadows claimed most of the dark stone hall. Stark silver and black banners hung on the walls. Only the distant flicker of torches cast dim, wavering light over the arched ceilings.

The castle seemed oddly empty. Samael must have thought that I'd never be able to get out of that room, because no one was patrolling here. The hallway opened into a curving stairwell that swept down to the front entrance, and there—without a single guard—stood an enormous oak door with iron filigree. It was just waiting for me to open it and run outside.

I took a deep breath. I didn't really know what I'd find on the other side of the door, but it would get me closer to freedom. Before I went into hiding, I wanted to see Mum again, to tell her what I knew. I wanted to see Zahra, too.

There was no sense in wasting time, so I picked up my pace, rushing down to the bottom of the stairs.

An iron bar locked the door. When I got to it, I stole a quick glance over my shoulder, making sure I was still alone. I heard not a single footstep in the halls. Slowly, I slid the bar across, trying not to make too much noise. With the door unbarred, I tried the handle. To my shock, it simply groaned open.

Just outside, a wooden bridge arched over the moat. The chilly night air swept over me, stinging my cheeks, and the icy ground froze my feet. Shocked at my freedom, I stared at the rambling, thorny garden that spread out toward the ruined iron fence. The gate stood open.

Beyond the fence, the river rushed past. I only had about a hundred meters to get to the gate, but I'd be out in the open while I did it.

It looked abandoned out here—a ruined stable to my left, and a roofless church to my right, overgrown with vines. Mist roiled off the river, which would give me a bit of cover as I escaped.

In the distance, I heard masculine voices. My breath frosted the air, clouding around my face. The cold bit at my toes, my fingers.

Now or never, Lila.

Gritting my teeth, I broke into a sprint over the wooden bridge, running through the winter air.

Freedom!

I had just made it to the end of the bridge when I slammed into a brick wall of pain. I froze in place, agony shooting up my bones. It felt like a magical poison was moving up my body, from my feet, up through my legs, into my belly. I grabbed my stomach, doubling over. I felt as if someone were carving me open and dipping me in boiling water at the same time.

Did I say I wasn't being tortured here? That was too hasty.

Shaking with pain, I staggered back. My legs were giving out, and I fell hard against the wood. My body convulsed, ignited with sharp pain from the inside out. I tried to roll onto my stomach, to crawl to the door. Was this how he was keeping me in here?

If I could make it back over the bridge, maybe the pain would stop. Once again, I tried to pull myself along, but I could no longer remember how my limbs worked.

I tried once again to push myself up onto my hands and knees, but my arms where shaking violently. Nausea rose in my gut, and I collapsed on the stone.

My mind started to go dark. I drifted off, my body going limp.

༺༻

I WOKE STARING INTO THE BEAUTIFUL BUT FURIOUS FACE OF the Angel of Death. Gold tattoos swept over his high cheekbones; fire simmered in his eyes.

Icy winter wind whipped over me, and moonlight silvered the side of his face. I was still outside, still lying on the wooden bridge.

And I was still in an extreme amount of pain.

Samael had lifted me by my shoulders, and he was staring into my face. His expression was murderous, though, frankly, I'd have welcomed death at that point if it would've stopped that magic poison.

I gritted my teeth, trying to remember how to form

words. "Take me inside, please. If it will stop the pain. Or I might throw up."

Wordlessly, Samael leaned down and scooped me up, carrying me over the threshold like I was a broken bride. As soon as we were within the castle walls, the pain subsided—completely. Now, my limbs felt supple and relaxed.

Taking a deep breath, I met Samael's gaze. His eyes smoldered intensely, and the air electrified around me. This was the first time I'd been close to another person in *months*. The warmth from his body radiated over my skin. Through his shirt, I felt his heartbeat. My flimsy nightgown was riding up, which meant one of his hands was pressed against my bare thigh.

Slowly, his gaze slid down, taking in the thin material of my nightgown. My hard nipples strained against the fabric.

Well, I certainly had his attention at last.

"Why are you in a nightgown?" he murmured.

"It's all I had. That and the food that arrives in the dumbwaiter." He'd completely forgotten about me, hadn't he? "Was that pain I just felt your way of trapping me in here?"

"Yes." A line formed between his brows, and his gaze continued to brush lower over my body, down over my thighs where the hem rode up.

"That was unpleasant." I was studying him closely—his dark eyebrows, the high cheekbones, the little dimple in his chin. The look he was giving me was *hungry*. I wanted to shriek at him about what I'd just experienced, but he looked like a starving man who wanted to run his mouth over every inch of me. And that was very distracting.

On my thigh, where his fingers gripped my bare skin, a sinful pleasure was rippling into my body. This was the addictive nature of the Fallen, with their seductive magic. Not to mention that I'd been starved for contact entirely. Slowly, a molten ache was building in me.

"Very unpleasant indeed," I repeated, but I sounded husky and breathless. "I am quite annoyed about it."

"Mmmmm ..." His voice was a deep, velvety vibration over my skin. "I am quite annoyed as well, since you tried to assassinate me and escape. I'd say *annoyed* is an understatement."

"The feeling is mutual."

And yet I was thinking of how it would feel to kiss his perfect mouth.

6
LILA

He released the powerful grip around my thigh, and I slid down his body, but he kept his other arm wrapped around my waist.

He spun me around so my back was to the cold stone wall and leaned down, whispering into my ear, "You're my enemy, and you will stay here where I can keep an eye on you. You are dangerous and untrustworthy."

I found myself wrapping my arms around his neck under his cloak. "You can't keep me locked in a room forever, Samael. I made one itty bitty mistake, but you're fine now, aren't you? Strong as ever. Time to move on."

"One *mistake?*" He leaned down, his breath warming the shell of my ear, and a shiver rippled over my body. "You have made many. You poisoned my soldiers with magic, you snuck out of the castle. You collaborated with the enemy, you tried to murder me and Sourial, and now you escape again. Looks like we need to talk about what *behaving* means. Don't we?"

"That's mostly just one mistake with lots of elaboration," I said breathlessly.

"Put your hands over your head."

My cheeks were growing warm. "Why, are you going to punish me?" Why did I *like* that idea? What, exactly, was wrong with me?

Maybe after all this time alone, I liked the full force of his attention on me, and I could see the desire in his eyes. His sensual, angelic magic was licking at my skin like a slow, erotic torture. So, I did as he commanded, and I raised my arms up against the chilly stone wall.

The look he was giving me sent molten heat sliding through my core. He gripped my wrists with one hand.

Pinning my arms to the wall, he leaned down, his mouth hovering over my throat. I was desperate for the contact, aching to feel his lips on me. I closed my eyes, arching my neck. *I'm ready for my consequences.*

Slowly, he brushed his lips over my throat, then his teeth. His tongue flicked over the pulse in my neck, sending a wave of hot desire coursing through my body. *God,* it felt good. I shuddered with pleasure. Pressed against the wall, I was completely vulnerable. And I wanted him bad.

His mouth continued to move over my neck. I ached for him. As he started to lift the hem of my skirt, a draft swept over my bare thighs.

"Samael," I whispered.

Were we in public now? I didn't really care. I just wanted his body against mine. It was like all those months of sitting alone in a room had crystalized into a sharp need for him, and only he could satisfy me now. Clearly, I had lost my mind.

I opened my eyes—and I stared into the face of death. Eyes of fire, swirls of golden tattoos. *Oh, God.*

Death incarnate.

My breath caught; my muscles went tense, my heart slamming against my ribs. That face wasn't meant to be seen by mortals.

He dropped the grip on my wrists and pulled away from me sharply, turning.

"That was a mistake." He pulled up his cowl, and I watched his fists tighten, knuckles whitening. "It won't happen again."

I was still catching my breath. "Agreed. A terrible mistake. As you mentioned moments ago, you loathe me."

"It was the nightgown." His voice was pure ice. "Any ordinary woman strutting around half naked, flashing her wares, would tempt a man."

"Any ordinary woman? Strutting around half naked? My *wares?*"

"Are you going to just keep repeating me?"

Holy hell. Now that stung. My cheeks burned, my stomach sinking. Suddenly, I forgot all about my escape attempt, the lacerating pain, and the ghost who'd tried to murder me. Somehow, this seemed like the worst thing to happen within the past hour.

I straightened, smoothing out my nightgown as if I could reclaim my dignity. I needed to say something equally stinging, to make him feel the slap of rejection.

"And I was only tempted by your stupidly, divinely beautiful face." Ah, there it was, the sharp sting of my rebuke. "Forget I said that. You only look good because I haven't seen another person in months. You know, there was a week there where I thought I would find a way to win you back. Then I came to my senses. You are arrogant and believe you're better than mortals. I still don't like you. You're not nearly as amazing as you think you are. You make everyone think of death. It's off-putting."

There. Dignity reclaimed.

"You should not have left your room," he said sharply. He turned, his eyes icy grey. The mournful look in them sent splinters of ice through my heart. "You'd be wise to let me forget you, Lila. You'd be safest that way."

"Safe from you?"

"You tried to assassinate the Venom of God. You're lucky to be alive, I think. The only thing keeping you from harm was staying in that room. I will come get you when I need you. Until then, you will remain in there. It is best for both of us."

Desperation rose in me, pure panic that I'd be stuck in that depressing room again. "I think there is some magic in that room trying to kill me. The ghost woman with the leaves. Was that you? Was that part of my punishment?"

"Ghosts again? Really?" He turned to walk away from me. "Oswald, my chamberlain, will return you to your room. I hope you understand now that you simply cannot escape. I gave you too much leeway in Castle Hades. I won't make the same mistake again."

"Wait, wait!" I shouted. My voice echoed off the stone walls.

He kept walking, pulling up the hood of his cloak.

"I might be going insane! " I shouted after him. Fatigue from the magic poison earlier still racked my body; I wasn't going to expend any extra energy unless I needed to.

At last, this made him stop. He stood quietly on the stairs, not looking at me. Just waiting, his cowl raised.

"I'm going mad in there. Inventing things." I hated how hysterical I sounded, but I couldn't face that room again. "I hear my name. I saw a woman in the reflection. She tried to choke me with leaves. She's either a ghost or I'm losing my mind. And neither of those things are great. I need to speak to other people. I need to get out now and then or I will be a raving madwoman. I promise you!"

His grip tightened on the railing. "It won't do for you to be insane."

"Good. I agree. It won't do at all. Look at that! We have so much in common. If you're going to keep me locked in your castle, I will need to speak to another person sometimes."

I sounded desperate, didn't I?

For the briefest of moments, he turned, sliding me a cold look. He drummed his fingertips over the railing. "The thing is, given the poor judgment you've already demonstrated, I'm not sure anyone would notice the difference if you lost your mind entirely. Would it be a loss to the world at all?"

I glared at him, trying to stay calm. My jaw tightened. "I can see that you're still angry, but I already apologized. And you *are* fine, aren't you? You don't need to belabor the point. Do you want a hair shirt and a public penance or something?"

"It would be a start."

What was he on his high horse about? "It's interesting to me, *Angel of Death,* that you have a moral problem with violence. I'm a bit perplexed by where you stand on that point, O slaughtering Venom of God."

"I never said I had a problem with violence. What matters is who you are killing, and if you have a good reason."

I arched an eyebrow. "And you've really never killed the wrong person during all these years? You never got bad information?"

"There is something about betrayal that I find particularly odious. And that is your nature. I carefully consider my actions. I take care to ensure that I am on the right path. That is why I consult my dreams. You act in uncontrolled rage. You have no training, are undisciplined, and act on impulse without carefully considering all angles. You're feral, like an animal. A common mortal trait, isn't it?"

My mind flickered with the memory of his True Face and the chains of fire writhing around him. "You think you're superior to mortals. But you forget I've seen your uncontrolled side, Samael. You'll have to come up with a better distinction between us than that. You want me to think that you have always carefully considered your actions? I know you're lying."

He cut me off sharply: "Oswald and Emma will keep you company tomorrow. They can show you the castle interior."

I hadn't escaped. On the other hand ... I made some progress. I would be meeting with people. Thank the stars, I'd have someone to talk to. This was an improvement.

He cast one last icy gray look in my direction. At that moment, I realized how badly I'd wanted his attention, even if I'd been arguing with him. For the past two months, I'd felt hollow, carved open. I'd take an argument over silence any day.

"In Castle Hades," he said, "you told me one night that you thought there was a ghost in your room, and that was why you got drunk. I believed you at the time. It was why you tried to escape—or so you said. It wasn't until after you tried to kill me that I realized you lied about a lot. And your whole plan was to seduce me so you could try to kill me for the Free Men. You feigned fear of ghosts that you do not believe in. So forgive me if I don't believe you about this new ghost in your room. But you can trust that you won't get the chance to try to kill me again. Apparently, you can pick a lock, so I will not bother with that. But you do understand if you try to escape the castle to get to the Free Men, you will feel the effects of my wrath."

"I'm not lying," I said. "This time."

He started climbing the stairs again.

"Samael, if I could, I'd be hunting down the Free Men with you, because they are the real enemy. I understand that now, and you must believe me. And you have to know I'm on your side! Because whoever the Baron is, he stole my best friend and my sister from me, and he turned them into monsters. I want to hunt him down, just like you do. And I want to go after Finn for the very thing you hate so much: betrayal. If you let me free, I will help you!"

I realized I was shouting at him mostly because I didn't want him to leave—because I wanted to see if he'd turn those pale gray eyes to me once more.

He paused once more on the stairs. "Soon, Lila, I will call on you for help. Soon, I will need you to marry me."

7
LILA

That ... was unexpected.

I felt as if I couldn't catch my breath. "Well, I am certainly flattered, but at the very least, you're supposed to look someone in the eye when you propose."

"It's not a real proposal, of course. This is the job I originally hired you for. You are still working for me, remember? The Council of the Fallen requires that I marry a mortal. You are the one in my dreams. Nightmares, really. You will play the part. That is all."

Leverage. That's what Ernald would say. It was all about leverage. He still wanted me to be his wife. "Is that why you don't want me to go insane? It would ruin the big show of a wedding if I was raving down the aisle?"

"Precisely."

I held up my hand. "I need a ring, of course. To show how deeply in love we are."

He frowned. "A ring?"

"It's what mortals do when they are engaged to be married. And when you're married, you get a second ring." I cocked my head. "You fell five hundred years ago. Have you not paid any attention to mortals during that time?"

"I avoid mortals as much as possible, and I intend to continue." With that final word, he stalked off into the shadows, leaving me alone once more.

My lip curled as I watched him prowl away.

Still, leverage was something. Now I knew why I was still alive. But the question was, what would he do when he didn't need me anymore? Once he was crowned king, he wouldn't need to keep me around.

Maybe I'd need to practice being nice to him, even though he *loathed* me and was infuriatingly condescending about mortals. I'd plaster a smile on my face and charm him.

As I started to climb the stairs, I heard footsteps echoing from the hallway above. A man with a slim build rounded the corner. He gave me a charming, crooked smile, his green eyes twinkling.

"Oswald, at your service." He bowed slightly. "Castle chamberlain." A little raven tattoo peeked out from under his collar.

So, he was a mortal like me.

I crossed my arms in front of my chest, unwilling to give him the same view I'd given Samael.

Leverage. The word took root in my brain.

All at once, it occurred to me that I could gain more freedom in this castle if the servants thought I was important.

"I am Lila, future countess. Engaged to the count. Did he mention that?"

Oswald's eyes sparkled. "I was, in fact, informed just moments ago. Congratulations. He has been very secretive about your presence here. I knew there was food going to that room, but not who it was for."

victim. They're the opposite of angels, who feel a lot. Rage. Love." He chuckled good-naturedly. "It's all very dramatic. I'm sure you know."

At last, we reached my little prison room. The door was still open from when I had escaped, certain freedom awaited me. Such an innocent time, thirty minutes ago.

"Thank you, Oswald. I look forward to seeing you and Emma tomorrow." But I paused in the doorway, not eager to rush back into the haunted room.

He gestured at the open door. "You'll be fine, my lady. Even if ghosts are real, they can't kill you. It's all illusions and tricks. Are you superstitious?"

"Oh, yes." I knocked on the stone wall three times. "I do that for luck."

"Then keep knocking, and find whatever makes you feel secure. It's all mind over matter."

I narrowed my eyes at him. I didn't entirely believe him, but I took a deep breath and stepped inside. A lantern stood on the dresser, and I flicked it on. Whether or not it was a fire risk, I'd be sleeping with the lantern burning.

When the doors shut behind me, I looked around the room, taking in the shadows that seemed to seep from the corners.

For a moment, I closed my eyes, remembering how it had felt to be so close to Samael. The pure power of his body. His heat radiating over me. I brushed my fingertips over my lips, imagining his lips grazing over mine. But as I did, an icy chill skimmed over me, the hair raising on the back of my neck. My eyes snapped open. I felt her here.

It was just me and the ghost.

8

LILA

I saw no signs of the ghost, but I thought I'd give her a warning anyway, in case she was still lingering around, invisible.

I held out my arms to the side. "All right, you phantom twat. I'm not scared of you. And I know that your whole purpose is to try to scare me, so you might as well just give up, because I do not care about you, and I never will. You can't kill me. You musty wanker."

The little speech seemed to actually work; I felt the fear leaving my body.

Exhausted, I crossed into the bathroom. I pulled off my nightgown and knickers, then turned the tap to start running hot water.

I shivered as I waited. The castle air was freezing. Moonlight poured in from the tall window in the bathroom, spilling over the small stone room. It held an iron tub, in which I washed my nightgown every other day.

Finally, the water filled the tub high enough, and I tested the heat with my fingertips. At least this would be a nice, much-needed distraction from my current debacle.

But just before I stepped into the tub, I glanced into the mirror, and my heart spluttered. The ghost I'd just called a musty wanker was behind me in the reflection. She stood with her arms outstretched, hands hanging down; her hair writhed around her head like snakes, her neck and spine bent at odd angles like they'd been broken. Her head lolled forward, her face in shadow and covered by hair.

My blood was arctic. "I'm not scared of you," I said quietly.

It didn't sound at all convincing.

Clenching my jaw, I whirled to face her.

But she was gone. It was just me and the steam rising from the bath.

Good. Just an illusion.

Then, when I chanced a look in the mirror again, a gap formed in the steam, which seemed to rise around a dark silhouette. Slowly, the ghost appeared again in the gap, and my stomach clenched.

Without warning, one of her bony hands shot out and grabbed me by the throat. She gripped my neck hard, then shoved me against the wall so hard a crack echoed through the room. Pain racked my body as I slid to the floor. I tried to stand again, but the ghost dug her fingernails in deeper.

Terrible gurgling sounds emitted from her throat. Strands of hair undulated before her face, covering her eyes. Rotten teeth jutted from her gums.

In a panic, I slammed my left fist into the side of her head, but it was like hitting an iron wall. Pain exploded through my knuckles.

For a ghost, this bitch was strong as hell. She grimaced, and she started rasping, *"Whore. God will give you dirt to eat. God will fill your mouth with decay."*

With her hand squeezing my throat, leaves filled my mouth, choking me. I couldn't breathe. Oh God, I couldn't breathe. I was suffocating on decaying earth and leaves, about to die, naked, on a bathroom floor. Frantically, I grabbed at her hair, like a drowning woman trying to grasp anything that would save me.

The ghost leaned closer to me, whispering in my ear. "Samael will never love you. When he gets what he needs from you, he will kill you."

The words echoed around in my mind, and I clutched her hair harder, forcing her head down like I was trying to drown her along with me.

And that was when she simply disappeared again.

All the leaves and muck in my throat disappeared along with her. Gasping, I fell onto my hands and knees, the cold stone biting into my skin. I clutched my throat, sucking in air, one glorious breath after another.

I would never take breathing for granted again. Breathing was glorious. Breathing was life. Air was everything.

But what the fuck was *she*?

Was she, like Oswald thought, a curse from someone who hated me? That could be anyone. Samael, Sourial. The Free Men, if they knew magic. Any of the Fallen. I was not well-loved these days.

Perhaps she was a punishment of sorts.

I crawled to the bath and turned off the water. It had overflowed completely, but I'd deal with that later. I didn't want a bath now. Nor did I want to stand and risk seeing my reflection in anything. Reflections were bad.

So instead of standing, I crawled, naked, on my hands and knees across the cold bathroom floor.

This night *might* be some kind of low point for me. My mind flicked back to Finn and Alice—the reason I was locked up here. Anger simmered, and I thought of what Samael had said about betrayal. Their betrayal had cut me open more deeply than anything.

Shivering, I crawled into bed and slid under the covers, finding the silk was soft and welcoming against my bare skin. Considering how hard I was still shaking, I wasn't sure I'd be able to sleep tonight.

I lay in bed for what seemed like ages, staring at the moonlight pouring in through the window.

I'd been so close to freedom.

I WOKE TO MORNING LIGHT STREAMING INTO THE ROOM. I'd been clutching the blankets up to my chin like a child. Warm, buttery sunlight spilled over the stacks of books, the banners on the wall, the mirror. In the light of day, it seemed safe and cheery in here. Already, I could smell the coffee and food in the dumbwaiter.

I threw off the covers, still naked, and crossed to the bathroom. I snatched my nightgown off the cold floor and pulled it on.

I shivered. I could still smell the rotten scent of the ghost in here—a dank, musty smell, like rotten marsh water.

I wanted to *prove* the ghost had been here, though. Something concrete ...

I crouched down, my gaze homing in on a strand of long brown hair on the stone floor. I picked it up to inspect it. But with a flicker of disappointment, I realized it was my own.

My stomach rumbled, and I rose to cross back into the bedroom. I slid open the dumbwaiter, delighted to find my breakfast. As soon as I pulled everything off—the silver domed tray, the pot of coffee, the mug—and closed the little wooden door, the dumbwaiter started creaking down again.

I narrowed my eyes at it. That didn't normally happen until after I'd eaten and put the dishes back.

Sighing, I poured myself a cup of steaming black coffee,

and set out the tray on the little wooden table by the window. When I pulled off the dome, I found fresh baked bread, melted chocolate, and strawberries. Already, my mouth was watering, and I sat down to start with the bread and chocolate. But as I ate, the dumbwaiter started creaking again. More breakfast?

With my mouth full, I crossed back to the dumbwaiter and lifted the door. This time, I found a stack of clothes—neatly folded dresses in a few colors—deep green, black, grey. When I pulled them out and unfolded them, I found they were long-sleeved, ankle length, made of thin wool. A stack of neatly folded underwear lay beneath them, and a small wooden box.

Quickly, I changed into one of the dresses. The soft material slid down my body. It felt warm and expensive, a thin cashmere. And thank God I had fresh undies to slip into, so I wouldn't have to keep up my miserable scrubbing routine.

In fresh clothes, I picked up the box and opened it. Inside, I found an acorn that had been fashioned into a simple string necklace.

I smiled at it. In Albia, acorns were ancient symbols of good luck, meant to ward off evil. A little note lay underneath it, and I unfolded it.

I bit my lip as I tried to decode the words. After a moment, I understood what it said: *To ward away evil*, and then underneath that, *To help you sleep*. The handwriting was elegant, almost feminine in its beauty.

Who knew? Maybe the acorn would work.

I tied it around my neck.

I *needed* it to work.

9
LILA

Just as I was finishing breakfast, a knock sounded on my door. I pulled it open to find Oswald standing next to a tall, beautiful woman with enormous hazel eyes and rich brown skin. She wore an ankle-length, sky blue dress, and an enormous cream lace collar encircled her neck. Her curly hair was pulled back into a bun, showcasing two elegant dangling pearl earrings. Rosy-gold makeup shimmered over her high cheekbones.

"Hi. I'm Lila."

She fluttered her eyelashes. "Pleased to meet you, Lady Lila. I'm Lady Emma Pradham, though there are many here who call me Seneschal."

Oswald's nose crinkled. "No one calls you that."

She straightened. "Well, they should. It is my most impressive title."

I frowned. "Sorry, what's a seneschal?"

"I run this castle," she said. "The finances, overseeing the servants, and so on." She narrowed her eyes at my neck. "Beautiful acorn."

I shot Oswald a smile. "Thanks. It's for good luck."

She turned into the hallway. "Well, you will certainly need that these days. Evil is everywhere. Come on." She nodded down the hall. "We'll show you around."

I followed them into the hall, toying with the acorn at my neck. Rays of sunlight slanted through the mullioned, peaked windows. So much nicer here during the day.

As we strolled from one room to another, I took in the beauty of the ancient castle. It was a much simpler layout than Castle Hades. In fact, it was basically four wings arranged in a square around a central courtyard. From each of the corners, a tower rose high, piercing the sky,

Oswald and Emma took me past the enormous kitchen, with wide ovens that must have been a thousand years old, and I met the people who'd been putting together my food. Many of the rooms were derelict, the furniture covered in sheets. Cloths covered the paintings. The place had a sense of faded grandeur, its glory lost to time, and a cloud of sadness seemed to pervade the air. We swept through a library—two floors of books, with arched ceilings painted blue and gold.

Despite the beauty all around me, my mind kept sliding back to everything that had happened last night—the hot encounter with Samael, the painful magic, the spectral attack. For some reason, I desperately wanted Samael to believe me about the ghost, but I understood why he wouldn't. That stupid lie I'd told in Castle Hades.

From the upper floors, I looked out through the old windows, warped with age. The thorny, untamed garden spread out over the courtyard, no longer cared for. I wanted to see it alive again. For just the briefest of moments, I thought I saw something shifting in it—the glimmer of green buds sprouting, coming to life before my eyes in the dead of winter.

"Lila?" asked Emma. "Everything okay?"

The illusion slipped away again.

Crikey, I was losing it. For a moment, I wondered if I'd made the buds appear, like I had at Castle Hades with the nightshade. But it was gone now. An illusion.

I blinked, clearing my head. "We have one more wing, don't we?"

Emma's eyes glinted. "The last one is my favorite."

As we walked, I kept glancing out the window, longing to see life out there.

In the final wing, Emma led us into a ballroom so large it could be a cathedral of gray stone. Diamond-pane windows stretched up twenty feet, letting the amber morning light pour over the floor. Chandeliers dangled from a soaring vaulted ceiling.

In the empty ballroom, Emma twirled in a circle, and the hem of her dress spun around her. "Someday, when all the fighting is over, we need to hold a ball in here." She stopped twirling and looked at me, her eyes shining. "You're one of the lucky ones. I've been alone in here far too long."

Oswald blew a curl out of his eyes and leaned against a column. "You have me."

She smiled at him. "And you're a lovely colleague, but I want a romance. Like Lila has."

My smile must have looked like a grimace. "True love. That's me."

Emma turned toward the window, stroking her lace collar. "When you are lady of this place, we should hold balls again, of course. I hope you can make Samael cheerier. He's been morose forever, I think. But I don't think it used to be like this. What do you think it was like in the days when Samael used to live here? I imagine it was much livelier." Her voice echoed off the high ceilings. "Music, dancing, masked balls. Everything."

I stared. When Samael ... used to live here? In the Iron Fortress?

Oswald folded his arms. "He just isn't the party type, is he? I doubt he was any more fun five hundred years ago."

"Hang on," I said. "What do you mean, 'when he used to live here?' He was here five hundred years ago?"

Emma stopped twirling and frowned at me. "It was built for him, a gift from one of the Albian kings for helping to suppress the northern rebellion. Have you never read a history book?"

I sighed. "No. I'm only just learning to read."

Emma's eyes widened. "Fascinating. So you just ... have to accept whatever people tell you as fact?"

"No ... everyone has to sift out truth from reality. Books can lie, too," I pointed out. "And even photographs, as I recently learned."

"Oh?" Emma was studying me closely, morning light washing over her. "You know, Samael told us that he would marry you, but he hasn't said why he locked you in a room by yourself. I know something happened at Hades Castle, but not what."

Good. They needed to think Samael and I were in love. "He's just making sure I'm safe for the wedding. Like you said, evil is all around us. But let's not dwell on that. When I am countess and overseeing this castle, we should bring the garden alive again. And we'll throw parties here. We can bring in musicians from the Bibliotek."

Her eyes widened again. "Wonderful! It has been infinite tedium in here lately. I think I will enjoy having you here."

"And as his future wife," I said, "I'd like to know as much about my home as I can. Every detail."

Oswald's gaze darted to Emma. "No."

Interesting. "No what?" I asked. "What are you saying no to?"

"There's a forbidden room." Emma's eyes danced with mischief.

Oswald glowered at her. "Emma loves going in it."

She shrugged. "It's not forbidden to the *seneschal*. I don't understand why it's forbidden at all. It's a mystery, isn't it? And I love a mystery. It is the one thing I have to entertain myself here. Except Oswald has no curiosity, dullard that he is. No offense, Oswald."

"Offense taken," he snapped.

I smiled. "Surely not forbidden to me, as the future Countess of the Iron Fortress."

"We're not going in," said Oswald. "Not without the count's permission."

Emma grinned. "Follow me."

10

LILA

We stood outside an ornate set of doors carved with the most fascinating symbols, some of them beautiful and some of them grotesque—gargoyles with their tongues sticking out, monstrous faces.

My gaze lingered over a carving of a moon wrapped in thorny vines. The vine leaves wrapped around another symbol: a raven wearing a crown.

The Raven King. I could almost feel his presence here, like in Castle Hades.

Now, I felt an overwhelming desire to see inside the room, almost like I'd find him in there. The ancient king's power thrummed through the door, and it was like an invisible cord pulling me in. I had to see what was in this room.

Emma pulled a set of long skeleton keys from her pocket. "Since you will soon be in control of the castle along with the count, I don't see why you can't have a quick peek in the mystery room."

"What if he returns early?" said Oswald. "We didn't get permission."

"Shh." She slid the key into the lock. "Stop worrying. Why would he hide things from his wife?"

"Exactly," I said. "He wouldn't." *Lie.*

When the door swung open, I was staring into an enormous bedroom, nearly the size of a ballroom. It smelled a bit musty in here, and the tapestries on the wall were old and threadbare, but the rest of the room was well-preserved. Windows reached from the floor to the towering ceiling, overlooking the thorny courtyard garden. The wind whistled in through broken windowpanes.

The room had a bleak atmosphere—all deep gray stone and dark wood furniture. A four-poster bed stood by one of the windows, with the curtains drawn before it. The pale silver bedspread looked worn with age. The room had a distinctly feminine presence: the delicate engravings in the stones depicting vines and flowers, the ornate silver stitching on the bedspread, a mahogany table with finely etched glasses and bottles of wine.

Not the Raven King, then.

Disappointing—and confusing.

I cleared my throat. "And why is this room locked? Who lived here?"

Oswald shrugged. "He won't tell us."

"And that is why I'm obsessed with this room," said Emma. "Because *why?* We don't get much excitement here, but this is a mystery."

"Is it not covered in the history books?" I asked. "There must have been someone living here when Samael was here five hundred years ago."

Emma sauntered across the room. "No, we only know the basics. The Iron Fortress was built for Samael as a gift, but there's no mention of angels at all in the books. It's always been a fraught topic in our country, one kept secret."

I bit my lip. "And who was the Iron Queen?"

Oswald shrugged. "You know our country is full of legends that aren't true." He flashed me a charming smile. "Not all of us share your superstitions."

I gestured at the room. "And yet here we are, in a locked room in the Iron Fortress that no one can explain, in a castle ruled by an angel."

Emma cocked her head. "I haven't heard this legend. The Iron Queen."

"Do you believe in ghosts, Emma?" I asked.

"No, but I'm still scared of them." She plucked a bottle of wine off the table. "Is this a ghost story? I'm going to be needing a drink for this. Does wine go bad after five hundred years?"

Oswald's pale cheeks were turning pink. "Is that really a good idea?"

"It's a terrible idea," said Emma, plucking out a corkscrew from a drawer. "My favorite kind of idea. And anyway—the future wife of the count should not be deprived of aged wine. Go on, Lila." Emma had now wedged the wine bottle between her knees to open it. "Tell me about the Iron Queen."

I sat at the old, faded vanity mirror and looked into the murky glass. Above the mirror was the same set of symbols—the moon with leaves stretching out to curl around a crowned raven. Sitting here, I felt a rush of the Raven King's power.

I glanced at the mirror again. "She was a mistress or wife of the king who ruled here. Do you suppose that could be Samael?"

"No," said Emma, popping the cork. "He's never loved anyone. Not till you."

I bit my lip, surprised at how much I wished that were true.

"The legend was, the king locked her in one of the rooms. And people said he loved her so much he didn't want her to ever leave." I frowned at myself in the mirror. "Which sounds like the worst sort of love. Because she went completely mad in captivity."

Emma poured a glass and handed it to me.

I took it from her and tentatively sipped. Shockingly, it actually did taste good, despite little earthy bits of sediment. It tasted of herbs and currants.

An uncanny feeling washed over me. *You belong here.* I felt as if I'd been in this room before, like I knew what I'd see when I opened the drawer—

A sharp curiosity compelled me to lean down and pull one of the dresser drawers open. And when I did, I found treasures: finely carved mahogany chess pieces, a gilt-frame hand-mirror with murky glass, silk scarves, diamond jewelry, and hair clips.

I slid one of the hair clips into my curls, tuning out the sound of the two others talking. I straightened my spine, elongating my neck. For a moment, I seemed to have the regal bearing of a queen. A dark smile curled my lips. *Beautiful.* Maybe I wasn't meant for the slums.

I took another sip of the rich wine and reached back into the drawer, plucking out a brooch shaped like a snake. Diamonds and rubies gleamed from its curves. But as I turned it over in my hands, the sharp pin stuck in my finger, drawing a bright red droplet of blood. For a moment, I simply stared at the tiny dome of red on my fingertip.

Then, I shook my head. What the hell was I doing?

I'd gotten lost in all this luxury for a moment. My gaze slid to the open drawer of chess pieces and jewels. All this opulence going to waste seemed criminal, now that I thought about it.

"Lila," Emma was saying. "You all right?"

"Yes, of course." I stuck my finger in my mouth. "Just pricked myself."

"I'm not comfortable with the drawers open," said Oswald, his skin pale.

I couldn't stop staring at the shimmering jewels in there. A moment ago, I'd been completely entranced by them. Now, I felt a sort of hollow anger. In Castle Hades, I'd seen all the wealth around me, but people were at least *using* it. Something about this flagrant waste made my jaw clench.

"All this has been here for centuries," I said quietly.

When I was a kid, I'd get so hungry that I'd fly into rages, and Mum would give me her food to calm me down. I remembered our neighbor, Annie, selling her body for pennies, and while she worked, she'd give her baby over to one of the street-crawlers to look after. And the baby would scream and scream with hunger, so I'd clamp my hands over my ears—

My hands were shaking now, as I held the brooch.

This was a sin.

"This shouldn't be here." My voice sounded low and furious.

"*We* shouldn't be here," said Oswald.

"Imagine all this wine going to waste," said Emma, pouring another glass for me. "Why waste it?"

"Exactly," I replied, my voice a sharp blade. "This is all a waste. What is the bloody point—"

I took a long, slow breath, remembering I was supposed to play a part. I wanted them to think I was on good terms with Samael.

Carefully, I schooled my features into a pleasant expression, then took a sip of the wine. "Well, I'm sure Samael has his reasons for keeping the room locked."

Emma stood and crossed behind me, cocking her head. "I think whoever lived here had a wonderful life. I don't see how you could go mad in here. I bet she had lovers every night, and wine, and delicious food. Music and intrigues. The castle is dull, but this room isn't, and that is why I like coming here."

"I imagine she had fruit tarts," I said, trying hard to hide the anger in my voice. "I saw one once in a window." And the gnawing hunger in my stomach had nearly driven me mad. "I saw a tart the size of your hand, with custard and berries, and a glaze on it that made it shimmer like a jewel. And perhaps she had coffee with cream and whiskey—"

I looked up and stopped at once. The rigid set of Emma's jaw, her gaze cast just over my shoulder, made my stomach clench.

I turned to see Samael in the doorway in his dark cloak, flames dancing in his eyes.

For the briefest of moments, fiery chains flickered around him. "What are you doing in here?" His deep voice trembled over the room.

Emma had hidden her wineglass behind her back. "I was showing your fiancée around, as you asked."

"I'd like to speak to her alone." A sharp blade undercut his velvety voice.

I sat, frozen, at the vanity table, watching as the two others crossed out of the room silently.

Samael prowled over to me, unclipping the jewel from my hair. He dropped it in the drawer, then slid it shut. "These things are not for you."

I yanked it open again. "They're not for anyone, which is a crime. You could sell them and feed an entire neighborhood."

"Interesting theory. This room is off limits to you."

I pulled out one of the carved chess pieces—the queen. "Why? Is it to do with the Iron Queen? Or the woman's ghost?"

"As a thief, I'd expect you to be better at lying. You'll need new material, Lila. The first time, it might have been creative, but now, I'm realizing ghosts are your go-to lie. Please try harder."

I seethed. "I'll have you know that I'm amazing at lying, thank you very much. It just so happens that I'm not lying. Is there something you wanted me to talk about?"

"Yes."

"You need my help?" My eyebrows crept up, and I sipped the wine. "My day is getting even better. Help with what? Are we going to plan our nuptials? I would like strawberries in the cake."

"My trail of the Free Men has gone cold," he said. "They're no longer passing on any information to Ernald now that his cover is blown. Where do I find your friend Finn?"

I felt a smile creeping over my lips. Perhaps I would get to leave here after all. And I'd get what I wanted more than anything—to hunt down Finn. "I will take you there tonight, Samael. I have a very good idea where he might have gone. But I'll need you to take that dreadful magic away. The one that makes me feel like I'm dying."

He cocked his head, frowning. "You *are* dying."

"What?"

"Mortals are always slowly dying; it's the definition of being mortal."

I pinched the bridge of my nose. "You and Sourial are a bit of a buzz kill with that *mortals are always dying* philosophy, you know that? We don't think of ourselves that way. Anyway, the important question is, do you have the power to lift that magic that makes me feel like I'm being ripped apart if I leave the castle?"

"Of course."

"Then I will go with you. I can lead you to the very spot where Finn would hide."

11
LILA

I opened the castle door with a flutter of nerves, worried for a moment that the spell wasn't lifted, and clutched the little bag slung over my shoulder. I'd packed it with a snack and a knife. I liked to be prepared, though there wasn't much I could do to prepare for that magic poison.

I took a tentative step onto the wooden bridge and pulled my cloak tighter around me, my muscles tense. Then, I took another. As I started walking across the moat, I felt no pain, and my body relaxed.

Samael stood by the river's edge outside the gate, a dark silhouette in the roiling mist. Under his cloak, I caught the glint of his sword's hilt. Whatever else happened, I was certain he wouldn't let me out of his sight.

The old iron gate rose on either side of him. With his cowl pulled up, he looked like he was trying to hide from the world, only his bright gray eyes shining out from the gloom. Fog billowed off the river.

In the distance, the somber tone of a ship's horn floated on the wind. Hard to believe I was actually about to get some freedom, to step out of this place.

I pulled my cloak tighter around me, taking a tentative step onto the path, waiting to see if pain would rip through my limbs. As I took one step after another on the crumbling stone path, I still felt nothing.

Just as Samael had promised, he'd released me from the spell—for tonight, at least. I felt a thrill of joy at being outside, even if it was freezing.

From under his cowl, Samael gave me a curious look. "What are you smiling at?"

"Several things. First, I'm finally getting to do what I need to do, which is to hunt down Finn and my sister."

"Ah, Finn, your dear friend who gave you the bomb to assassinate me. You must miss him."

"*Former* friend," I corrected.

But I did sort of miss him. At least, I missed the friend I'd *thought* I knew.

"We'll see about that." Samael reached into his cloak and pulled out a simple gold ring. "Here, the jewelry you requested." He grabbed my hand and dropped it into my palm.

I shook my head. "No, Samael. You're supposed to slide it onto my finger. Really, you should be on your knees."

His lip curled in a slight smile. "I kneel for no one."

I handed the ring back to him. "Slide it on my finger and look me in the eye when you do it."

"Is this really necessary?"

"Oh, absolutely. We are, after all, deeply in love."

His icy eyes narrowed, but he held my gaze as he slipped the ring onto my ring finger. It fit perfectly, gleaming in the dim light. I held it up closer to my face, noticing words engraved in the gold—Angelic letters.

"What does it say?" I asked.

"It says you deserve death, and I have been far too kind."

I glared at him. "That's a lot of words to fit on a little ring."

"Tell me where to find Finn."

I started walking, and the wind rushed over the river, toying with my cloak.

Samael shot me another sly look as we walked. "What's in your bag? Do I need to search it for bombs?"

"A knife."

"Of course. You stole it from the kitchen, I imagine."

"They have plenty. But more interesting than the knife is what Oswald gave me. An acorn necklace, to ward off the evil, and a fruit tart because I said I wanted one. Do you want to see it?"

"I have seen pastries before."

"It is a true mortal-made wonder. If it doesn't make you reevaluate the superiority of mortals over angels, then your mind is broken beyond repair." I reached into my bag and pulled out a tart wrapped in wax paper. The paper had smudged the glaze a bit, but it still looked glorious. "What have angels ever done for the world that rivals this sublime art?"

His jaw tightened. "Do you plan to eat it at some point, or compose poetry about it for the rest of the evening?"

My stomach rumbled. "Oh, I've been saving it to eat on our walk. I haven't wanted to destroy it. I'm enjoying the anticipation too much." I held the tart up to the moonlight, and silver light glistened over the glazed berries. "But honestly, have you ever seen anything so lovely?"

When I lifted my gaze, I found his gray eyes piercing me. "I have."

I tucked the tart into my bag. "I'd share it with you, but I'm not sure you deserve it."

"Why not?"

Because you said any half-naked woman would catch your eye. "Because you're a bit evil."

As I led him down a winding road of crowded brick buildings, he fell silent. We turned onto a crooked street that jutted off from the river walkway, leading us up into the East End. The street meandered northward between crooked tenements. Warm lights beamed from some of the windows.

Dark brick walls rose on either side of us. Someone had painted *The Storm is Coming* on one of the walls, with an eye above it, and a lightning bolt beneath it. I pointed at it. "Free Men propaganda."

"You can read now?"

I smiled. "I've been practicing. And Emma helped me more today."

He stared at the graffiti. "Their movement is growing faster every day."

"You're helping it grow."

"I'm *what?*" A harsh edge undercut his voice.

"Don't you think they might be fighting a propaganda war?"

"I don't care what their methods are. I plan to kill them all so they stop."

"But they will keep growing if people think they're right. The public executions, the bodies hanging from the castle walls—all that will make their numbers swell. The people in Dovren don't know that the Free Men are murderers. They've done a good job of framing you for killing those women, and they're winning the propaganda war. All people see of you is you cutting off heads in the town square. It doesn't make you seem nice, exactly. How much do you think that is helping you win them over?"

"I wasn't trying to win them over. I was trying to scare them into submission."

"When people are desperate and starving, they forget to be scared."

"The reality of this world that mortals have created is that you can kill or be killed. That's the world you've made. You've left each other to starve. Someone has to take control, and if I can't be loved, I will be feared." His low, reverberating voice sounded dredged from darkness. "If I don't stop the Free Men, they will burn this country to the ground in the Night of the Harrowing. I will not stop this through *love*." His final word dripped with disdain.

"You said 'if I can't be loved.' Why can't you be loved?"

Shadows seemed to gather around him. "I'm the Venom of God. I was made for vengeance and death. Don't try to make me into something I'm not. In your words, I'm a bit evil."

I supposed I couldn't argue. The street we walked now opened into a park, where a lone, sparse tree clawed at the night sky. To the right, lights beamed from some brick buildings—abandoned factories that people had taken over as homes. To the left, train tracks ran over dark archways.

Samael's hand twitched at the hilt of his sword. He seemed edgy, tense. "Why do I feel like you're bringing me to my death here?" he asked quietly.

"Your death? First of all, you're immortal. Second of all, I could not take you in a fight." Though, for some reason, I liked the thought of trying.

I had to admit, I enjoyed the fact that I unnerved the big, bad Angel of Death.

I pointed at a rickety structure that was held up on stilts high above the train tracks. "That's where we're heading."

The tiny, ramshackle shack had once housed one of the train controllers used to operate the switches. Abandoned long ago, it had made a perfect hideaway for Finn and me as kids. He'd go there whenever he wanted to get away from his mum for a bit, which was often. I didn't know that Finn had definitely gone there, but there was a good chance.

"The old house on stilts," I murmured. "I know it looks grim, but I promise I won't try to murder you."

We passed the dark archways, which always unnerved me. All kinds of unsavory things happened under those old arches beneath the tracks. A soft rain started to fall over us.

"Are you going to tell me what exactly the Free Men have planned?" I asked to fill the silence.

With his cowl pulled up, Samael seemed to be hiding, cloaked in shadows. "I'll tell you only what you need to know."

Frustration simmered. What could I do to convince him that we were on the same side? I whirled, grabbing him by the arms. He peered down at me, and I stared directly into the icy gray eyes under his hood. I was so close to him I could feel the heat rippling off his body.

"Samael, I'm not part of the Free Men. If I saw Finn now, I'd try to kill him." Darkness was spreading in my chest as I realized I'd loved Finn, once, as a friend, but the old Finn was dead to me. "I trusted Finn, but he betrayed me. So did my sister. You're an angel. Can't you bloody tell when someone is being sincere? Is that not one of your powers?"

At last, Samael pulled down his cowl to give me a rare view of his perfect face—the high cheekbones, the markings. He had a strangely innocent gleam in his eyes, like he was trying to work out the world before him. He studied me for almost a minute, looking like he was trying to decipher me.

At last, he said, "All right. I believe you, Lila. About the Free Men, that is. I'll never believe you about the ghost. Now release my arms."

My chest unclenched, and I let go of him. "Good enough. We can work together, then."

Flames danced in his eyes, making a shiver run over my skin. "But you should know, Lila, that I wasn't lying when I said you were safest in the Iron Fortress. For one thing, as long as you're out here with me, you're at risk. I can kill mortals easily, but a horde of demons is a challenge even for me."

I turned to walk again with a rising sense of dread. "What demons are we talking about?"

"The Free Men have a book that will allow them to control demons." He cast a look behind him. "Then, they plan to summon a powerful, evil demon named the Harrower. Sower of Chaos. Sower of Death. Sower of Nightmares."

I shuddered. "That is a lot of sowing responsibilities."

"Demons are soulless creatures that can be used as weapons if someone knows the right spells. They feel nothing and have no emotions. They're easy to manipulate but destructive beyond measure. The Harrower is one of the worst."

"What do they want to use the demons as a weapon for, specifically? To kill angels?"

"Not just angels. They want to slaughter the mortal women who consort with angels, and the nephilim offspring. Anyone who works for us, like the servants they slaughtered in Castle Hades. They call it the Night of the Harrowing, the great purification."

Sickness churned in my stomach. "I can't believe Alice is involved in that shit. So the Harrower is their greatest weapon?"

"The Harrower is unique among them—a demon who can create more demons from the earth itself. They think chaos is an opportunity for their horrific vision to come to pass, and they will strike a deal with the worst demons to make sure it does."

I took a deep breath. "Okay. So we're up against some very nefarious characters."

"But that's not the only thing putting you in danger."
"What else?"

He kept his gaze focused straight ahead, no longer looking at me. "Me. I'm a danger to you."

12

SAMAEL

Lila frowned. "I thought we agreed we're on the same side for now."

"We are. But I'm not the same as when you first met me. I'm enjoying things again. Food. Alcohol. Light. And killing. That's the reaper side of me, the one who delights in death. Centuries ago, as a reaper, I killed with abandon, and I enjoyed it. I left villages full of the dead." Hazy memories flickered through my mind, dirt paths running with blood. "After angels fall, we are corrupted versions of our former selves. Ever since I nearly died, the corruption has been worse."

She stared at me, dark eyes piercing. Her hair whipped in front of her face. "But you won't hurt me."

"How do you know?"

"I can't explain it, but I just know."

Lila wanted me to be something I wasn't—an angel who'd never fallen.

I shrugged slowly and pulled out a flask, taking a sip. What I would not be telling her was that it wasn't just about violence. I was also thinking about the absolutely depraved things I'd like to be doing to her right now, starting with pulling her into one of these dark archways and ripping her dress off. I wanted to tease her body into uncontrollable desire, make her gasp and moan. I wanted to make her mine completely—to fuck her hard up against a wall while her fingernails clawed down my back. I wanted her nipples in my mouth, my cock inside her.

This was not the angel I'd been for centuries. This was a beast I wasn't sure I could control.

I had lied to her completely when I told her I'd be attracted to any woman strutting around half naked in front of me. That wasn't remotely true. But of course, I wasn't about to bare my soul to a woman who had used seduction to try to kill me. My instincts were correct, since she had told me I was evil, and that she didn't like me. Once this little excursion was over, I'd return to avoiding her.

She bit her lip, looking at me from behind a lock of brown hair. "Has it occurred to you that maybe you're fighting your true nature too much? Maybe that makes it worse."

"Are you saying I should just give in and enjoy an orgy of bloodlust?"

"No, but maybe you're not meant to be a virgin forever."

My mouth opened and closed in surprise. It almost felt like she'd been reading my mind. "You have no idea what you're talking about."

"Do you know what a constrictor knot is? If you struggle against it, it only gets tighter on your wrists. Maybe that's what you're doing. If you fight against your desire, maybe it gets worse."

A constrictor knot ...

My blood heated as I thought of *her* tied up in my bed, stripped naked and writhing.

But before I could respond, a burst of flames erupted in the distance. In the dark park that stretched out to our right, fire blazed beneath a gnarled tree. Something was on fire. It looked like an angel with wings of flames, dangling from a branch. Violent shouts rose around it.

"What *is* that?" asked Lila.

"An angel effigy. Of me, probably."

"Definitely losing the propaganda war."

A cold shudder rippled through my body when I thought of the Harrower rising again.

On the left, there was more graffiti on another wall, reading *Albia Will Rise Soon—Albia First.* Another lightning bolt had been painted beneath it.

"On the Night of the Harrowing, the streets will burn with demon-fire," I said. "They look forward to their doomsday. Those who helped the Free Men will be evacuated. The rest will perish. I've seen their vision in my nightmares—every alley filled with the nephilim dead, mortals among them, angels, too, the air scorched with flames. Anyone who tries to stop the purges will hang from nooses as traitors. They are selling it as a day of freedom, but it will be hell on earth."

"The Free Men hate angels, but they're fine living with demons?"

He shook his head. "No. They have a book of magic called the Mysterium Liber. It will allow them to control the lesser demons. So, when the demons are done and corpses fill Dovren, the Free Men will force the demons to kill themselves. Carve out their own hearts. Then, they will kill the Harrower. So, I have to kill the Harrower before any new demons are grown. As king, I will lead the Fallen to hunt the rest of the Free Men down, one by one."

"But how do we find this Harrower?"

"You'll help me, one way or another."

13

LILA

Dark and cryptic. I supposed that was typical for Samael. "Okay, well, I will do my best to help you find this Harrower, then."

A flicker of movement caught my eye. Instinctively, I started to reach for my knife. But the creature who crawled from the darkness wasn't dangerous at all. In fact, she was a little girl, clutching a small wooden tray of wilted boutonnieres.

The girl was barefoot and wore an old gray frock. She was pale and gaunt, her brown eyes too large for her face. One side of her jaw was swollen, which told me she'd once worked in the match factory. I'd worked there as a kid, but not long enough for the sulfur to affect me that way.

She shot Samael a nervous look. "Boutonnieres!"

He sheathed his sword and started to walk again, ignoring her completely.

"Wait, Samael," I said.

He went still, his back to us, blending into the shadows with his cowl raised.

I leaned down to look at her flowers. Daisies, corncockle,

bluebells, foxglove—common but beautiful flowers. The boutonnieres themselves were poorly made, the ribbons tattered and tied in bulky knots, falling apart. But the bluebells were a nice touch, and the overall effect was sweet.

"How old are you?" I asked the girl.

"Ten." She was the size of a six-year-old—probably severely malnourished. Her wrists looked like they could snap in half at any moment.

"What's your name?"

"Hannah."

I straightened, guilt cutting through me. I couldn't exactly walk past with the fruit tart in my bag now, could I?

I reached into my bag and pulled out the tart, unwrapping it. "Are you hungry?"

She stared at it, wide-eyed, almost like she couldn't believe it was real.

"I just need to know what it tastes like. The rest is yours." I broke off a little piece for myself, then handed her the rest. She gripped her tray with one hand, then grinned as she took the tart from my palm.

My stomach rumbled, loudly, and I stuffed the little corner of the fruit tart into my mouth. Sweet, creamy, tart—the taste exploded in my mouth. *Heaven.* I glanced over to see Samael watching me closely, so I shrugged. "I'm a thief, not a saint. Oswald gave that to me, and I have no idea if I'll get another. I had to see what it tasted like."

The little girl stared at her tart in awe, nearly dropping the tray. Then, she stuffed it into her gob. A few crumbs rained onto her tray from her mouth. It was only then that I noticed the dark bruise around one of her eyes.

My gaze flicked to her tray of wilted flowers. Whoever she lived with probably beat her if she came home empty handed. I didn't have anything besides the tart, though.

"Samael. You wanted some boutonnieres, didn't you?"

He turned to look at me, frowning. Confusion shone in his pale eyes. "Have you lost your mind?"

The girl stared at me, still chewing.

"You did want them. For our wedding. You can dry them, you know. Give them to the groomsmen. I think you need all of them. And she needs to sell them, of course, or she will have a very bad night. So it seems like a happy coincidence for everyone that we ran into each other."

Samael's brow was furrowed, the moonlight glinting off his pale eyes. He was studying me, perplexed. Then, he turned abruptly and strode over to the girl.

He reached into his cloak and pulled out a small bag, which was probably full of more coins than she'd earn in a lifetime. I thought he probably had no clue how much anything was worth, but I wasn't about to point it out. He gathered all the boutonnieres in one hand and stared at them.

The little girl dropped her tray and yanked open the bag of coins. "Fuckin' hell. That's a lot of money!"

She was a terrible negotiator. I crouched down to her level. "You should know that he's the count, and if anyone tells you the count is a terrible murderer, you remember this and tell them he's not all bad. He has his reasons for what he does."

She clutched the coins close to her chest, staring at me wild-eyed. Then, she ran back into the shadows, her tray forgotten.

When I turned back to Samael, I found him still staring at the boutonnieres, baffled.

I plucked one of them from his hand. "Here, let me help you. I can fix you up a bit.

"Do I need fixing up?" Samael grumbled. "I was under the impression I was stupidly, divinely beautiful. I believe that was your adverb-heavy phrase."

My cheeks flamed. "As I said, you were the first person I'd

seen in months. Your face is frankly mediocre. Average. As far as I'm concerned, you barely have noticeable features. It's just a blank expanse of tedium." This was perhaps the most ridiculous lie I'd ever told, and I was surprised he didn't burst out laughing.

Instead of laughing, his jaw tightened. The air seemed to grow cold and thin. "Mediocre." He spat the word out like it was a curse. "*Average.*"

Of course, he had literally no sense of humor about himself. I was getting to him, which delighted me. After all, he'd already dismissed me as *only as interesting as any woman who strutted around half naked*. Right after we'd kissed, no less. It had been *extremely* insulting, and he deserved to be rankled.

I finished fastening the flower to his cloak. "I said what I said. There. Now you have something interesting about you at last."

The air grew even colder around us. His eyes narrowed, and he went quiet for a moment. The wind toyed with his dark hair. "I think you want me. Someday I will get you to admit it."

"You first. Am I as interesting as any ordinary woman strutting around showing off her wares?"

He leaned down, whispering into my ear. "The Venom of God never yields."

The feel of his magic so close to me made a shudder run over my body. "The Venom of God needs to stop talking in the third person. It's not going to make you less average." I could feel his fury rippling over me. I had the sense that I was playing a dangerous game, but I couldn't stop myself. "When I saw you, I was like a man released from prison after ten years who shags the first ordinary hag he sees."

Shadows whipped around him, seeping into the air. "Is that right?"

I shrugged. "Absolutely. But everything is better with

flowers, even the Venom of God." His powerful magic thrummed up my spine. "Flowers have their own meanings in Albia. You see that bluebell? They're connected to angels."

"As an actual angel, I can confirm that is absolute bollocks."

"Daisies are for innocence," I went on, ignoring him. "Corncockle means an invasion, which I suppose is appropriate for you. This whole thing is really perfect for you. And now you have a nice pop of color in your ensemble."

"Just what I've always wanted. A *color pop* on my ensemble." He stared down at the boutonniere, then met my gaze. "I am an ancient creature of slaughter. In what possible way am I innocent?"

I shrugged. "You just are. The world confuses you. But you're also a dour, cranky weirdo with fire eyes, and the flowers will help you look more normal. Now I'm no longer as embarrassed to walk the streets of Dovren with you."

He frowned. "That's really how you'd describe me?" Without waiting for a response, he turned, stalking swiftly away. He was certainly rankled.

I caught up with him under one of the dark arches that led to the stairwell. "See? Dour and cranky."

"If you wanted that tart so badly, why were you compelled to give it to that misshapen wretch?"

"Because she's just a kid. Her face is swollen from the match factory. I saw that a lot when I worked there. And I remember what it was like to be starving. I remember when I was so hungry it was all I could think about."

He stopped abruptly, turning to me with something like anger in his eyes. "When I arrived here there was, and continues to be extreme wealth among mortals. The mortal aristocrats have as much wealth as I do."

I sucked the last bit of custard off my thumb. "Yes, but my neighborhood is full of people who don't have enough money for food. It has been since before you arrived. It's always been that way. Those bunters who lift their skirts in the park for a few pennies—do you think they're doing that for fun?"

"I've never thought about them one way or another."

"Well, color me shocked."

His features softened a little. "So, was your life like that? Were you out in the street barefoot trying to sell poorly made bunches of weeds?"

"I always had something on my feet, though I'm not sure you could always call them shoes. I had the same jobs she does. The match factory. Selling flowers. Selling bones I scavenged. Mud-larking—selling coins and other trinkets snatched from the river muck. I was always hungry, obsessed with food. I thought about it all the time. I dreamt about it. I wanted to steal it, but I was scared of hanging. I told my sister stories about what I'd eat if I had money. I'd pretend to be a princess living in a palace made of cake, surrounded by rivers of chocolate. Then I started working for Ernald. That was a step up."

Our footsteps echoed off the walls, and we started climbing the stone stairs.

"But how often were you fed?" he asked. There it was again, that anger.

My jaw tightened. "Why are you so interested in this?"

"I honestly have no idea."

"I know plenty of mortals have wealth. But you have more money than God. You are precisely the kind of person who could fix that situation. If you spread it out a bit, the Free Men would have a much harder time convincing everyone that you're monsters. They'd look like the wealth hoarders."

He slid me a sharp look. "Why would anyone buy bones?"

I wasn't sure I was getting my point across. "To make

soap. Anyway, does it bother you if people in the city you rule are starving?"

"I can't care about everyone. I would lose my mind if I did. You have to choose what to care about, or you go insane. I have seen one generation of mortals after another die before my eyes. Your lives are over in the blink of an eye. I can't get attached. If their suffering bothered me, I'd be raving by now. But I suppose I care if some people are hungry."

At the top of the stairs, we rounded a corner to the elevated train tracks. High above us loomed the house on stilts. Craggy black poplar trees grew beneath it, their branches bare. I stared up at it, feeling pressure in my chest when I thought of Finn as a boy, showing me this place.

Samael crossed to the base of the ladder and motioned for me to go first. I hadn't been here in ten years maybe, and it looked even more dilapidated than the last time I'd come with Finn. I started climbing the old wooden ladder. It felt soft, half rotten under my fingertips.

The icy night wind whipped over me, tearing at my hair as I climbed higher. But when I was near the top, a rotten rung broke beneath my feet with a snap.

I started to fall.

14

LILA

There was only enough time for my heart to pound hard once—then Samael's powerful arm caught me in the air.

One arm wrapped around me, then the other. His wings spread out behind him. As he held me close against his chest, I stared at his dark wings, the feathers shot through with veins of gold. They gleamed against the night sky.

With his wings beating the air, I stared at him. This close to his divine beauty, my heart raced. He was the literal opposite of ordinary, and I was shocked he didn't know that.

I wrapped my arms around his neck as we swept up higher, to the rickety house.

Once in the doorway, I slid down his body, trying not to think too much about how good it felt to be this close to his power, the warm steel beneath his soft clothes. I lingered near him for just a moment longer than I should have. When one of his hands traced down my side, grazing my waist and hips, heat raced in its wake.

My pulse was racing. I reminded myself of what he'd said about me—any woman strutting around flashing her wares.

That would be my mantra.

I stepped away from him, and he pulled up his cowl once more, hiding.

As I looked around the old house, there was a pit in my stomach. Once, this place had been a refuge. Nostalgia pierced me as I breathed in the scent of old wood, the moss that grew along the windowsills. It was only one room—nearly empty. But just as I'd expected, I saw the signs that Finn had been here. His pillow lay on the floor, and a pile of blankets. A candle and a few books.

I turned around, my eyes stinging. This place was taking the decades away; suddenly, I was eight again. Sun was beaming through the windows, and people were playing in the park outside.

"Finn used to pretend to be a lord," I said, my throat tight. "He'd put on a fancy accent and call himself Lord Finnothy Dexter. I thought it was just a dumb kid game. I guess he really wanted to be one of them. Someone with a moneyed accent, ruling the city. I thought it was a game."

Cold wind whipped in through a broken windowpane. I crossed to it, looking out at the burning effigy—a bright pinpoint of flame in the darkness. A small mob had formed around it, screaming. *"The Storm is Coming!"*

"Do you think these are his things?" Samael asked from behind me.

"I recognize the blue felt pillow. But he won't come back now. He'll notice the broken ladder." I knelt. "The floorboards. That's where he hides things. Do you see a raised bit of wood anywhere? Anything that looks a little different to the rest of the floor? Or hollow?"

Samael knelt, and within moments, he was pulling up a floorboard. Then, he extracted a piece of paper. When I crossed to his side, I peered over his shoulder at a white card with handwriting on it.

My reading was too slow, and I was impatient. "What does it say?"

"Where we beat the walls with sticks, two monstrous giants flank the door," he read. "Under the ground, the ancient stones lay sleeping. Once, the bear's blood ran down upon us. Below us, Albia sleeps, ready to rise again. On the day of the slain wolf, we meet at sunset." He stared at it. "Does this make *any* sense to you?"

I pulled the card from his hand, and as I did, my fingertips brushed against his. With just that one brush of contact, erotic heat shot through my fingers, into my body. Stupidly addictive.

He looked unnerved for a moment, then ran his hand through his hair, turning away. "What does that nonsense mean?"

"I think I know what this is. There's an old Great Hall in the oldest part of Dovren, and it's been used for trials for centuries. Above the entrance, there are statues of two giants —Gog and Magog. There's an old legend that they founded Dovren."

"So, the Free Men are meeting in this hall. Considering they're in hiding, that seems absurdly risky, doesn't it?"

"Beneath the Great Hall, there's an ancient temple. It's quite amazing, actually. This is what is wonderful about Dovren. You're walking along on what looks like an ordinary street, full of smoke and fog and fish vendors, but beneath you is thousands of years of buried life. The old temples, the ghosts of the past. When magic used to be alive."

He turned back to me. "I am enjoying your enthusiasm, but are you going to get to the point?"

"At low tide, you can get to a door in an embankment wall next to the river. It's an amazing place. Long ago, they held rituals in the temple there, when they worshipped the old gods. A person would stand beneath the earth, and they'd slaughter a bear above them, and the blood would run down to the worshipper, purifying them in power. Back before we killed all the bears."

He arched an eyebrow, and that was all he needed to do to convey something like *mortals are violent maniacs*.

"Well, it was a long time ago," I said defensively. "Anyway, that's where they plan to meet. The underground temple."

He hadn't stopped staring at me. "Any idea when?"

"The day of the slain wolf." I cleared my throat. "We used to have wolves, also, before they were all slaughtered. There's always a party in the old temple on Wolfshunt Day. They'll be blending in with the crowd. It seems to be one of their favorite ways to meet."

"So, there is a day when your kind commemorates the slaughter of an entire species."

"I know, it's terrible. But there are nice festivals in Dovren, too. There's a day they give cakes to widows"—I swallowed—"whose husbands were executed for stealing food. You know what? Let's stay focused. On Wolfshunt Day, people dress in their best gowns and suits, and wear masks of wolves or other forest animals. Some people dress head to toe in straw and dance around. The crowd pretends to hunt a wolf, and we choose a Winter King. It's... tomorrow, I think. It would be easy enough for us to go in disguise. I can keep an eye out for Finn or Alice. We can take Finn captive for more information. Then we can find out more about the plan to summon the Harrower."

"I have an entire army at my disposal. We could capture everyone there."

I shook my head. "They won't all be Free Men. Some of them will be children, on their happiest night of the year. They get apples, candy. A chance to run wild. I've been nearly every year. The Free Men are using innocent people as cover."

He studied me carefully. "You've been every year?"

I nodded. "I'd never miss it—" A feeling of unease stopped me from finishing my sentence. The hair stood up on my nape, and I felt a malign presence spilling through the room. "Samael."

He was already at the window, peering outside. "They're here." His voice was a low rumble that slid through my bones.

"Demons?" I whispered.

"Yes."

A chill rippled up my neck, and I turned to look out into the darkness. The breath left my lungs. The demon seemed to come from the night itself, a woman with midnight hair and pearly white skin, lips red as blood. The most terrifying thing about her was her eyes—black as jet, no irises. Gleaming and empty.

Soulless.

Ice slid down to my bones as I stared into the face of pure evil.

Then, three more appeared behind her, just like her. My heart slammed against my ribs as I took in the bows they carried, arrows aimed at us.

They'd found us already.

15

LILA

Samael slammed me hard against the ground, the full force of his weight pressing down on me, his heavy sword resting against one of my legs. The breath had left my lungs with the force of the blow. I stared up into the face of death, golden tattoos sweeping over his cheekbones, celestial fire burning in his irises. Something was jutting into my ribs below my breast.

My breath shuddered, and I wondered why he wasn't getting off me. I touched his back and felt blood, and a wooden shaft.

That was when I realized what was jabbing into my chest—the tip of an arrowhead. It had slammed clean through Samael's body, protruding through his ribs and into mine.

Bloody hell. "Are you okay?" I whispered.

He clenched his jaw and pushed himself off me. Sitting on the floor, he turned his back to me. "Rip it out. I can't reach it."

Another arrow slammed into the wood, splintering it. I didn't *love* the idea of pulling a bolt of wood out of another living person, but there wasn't much time to mess around here. So, I pressed my feet against him for leverage, gritted my teeth, and pulled.

The arrowhead seemed stuck on a rib or something, and I tried to block out the horror of the situation. The *noise* the bolt made as I pulled it out was something I hoped to forget as soon as possible, and blood poured from his back. As soon as the bolt was out, he rose and stormed out the door. He leapt into the air, wings erupting behind him.

I watched as he soared, then arced away. A menacing magic floated on the wind, making goosebumps raise on my arms.

My heart hammered, and I crouched down beneath the window. I closed my eyes. *Raven King, give me strength.*

I should stay out of range. As an immortal, Samael could look after himself.

But I had to see what was happening out there, so I stole a glance over the top of the windowsill.

Samael moved with such stunning speed I could hardly track him—just the silver blur of his sword as it cut through a demon's head. Her body plunged to the ground, and inky blood spilled out over the soil. And yet ... her body continued to twitch, her eyes fluttering.

As he flew for another demon, an arrow slammed into Samael's shoulder from the front. Blood streamed, making me wince. My heart skipped a beat. There were more of them coming for us now. One of them had lifted her arrow to me. I ducked down again.

But I didn't feel much safer in here. A chill rippled over my body. A second later, a demon whipped past the open doorway, searching for me but not yet seeing me, her dark magic spilling into the room.

Raven King, give me strength.

It was almost as though I heard his answer in the hollows of my mind; a low, knelling voice: *Buried life lay under this city.*

I could harness it. I had before, hadn't I? I just had no idea how.

The demon swept past again, circling the small shack. I had the disturbing sense that Samael could be in trouble, that I had to get to him. He couldn't be killed, but the Free Men would love to torture him into insanity.

My breath was ragged in my throat, and I whirled, trying to track her. She whipped around again, pausing before the doorway, finally seeing me. Her black eyes sent ice through my veins. I gripped my knife, not willing to throw it yet. Power moved through the wood, into my legs.

The demon raised her bow and loosed the arrow. I shifted just in time, and it skimmed my thigh, pinning my dress against the wall.

Lightning fast, she unleashed another arrow that grazed my other thigh. It pierced the other side of my dress, drawing blood. Panic started to crackle through my body.

I was trapped.

An unearthly demon cry keened behind me, eerily like a victory whoop.

Panic surged now—for Samael, for myself. I was starting to get the sense they wanted to take us alive. And considering they carved out people's lungs, I didn't want to know what they'd do with us.

As the demon nocked another arrow, time seemed to slow down. Anger and a need to protect Samael overwhelmed me. And along with it, something far darker. Ancient.

Power thrummed up my legs, vibrating through my body. Time had slowed to a crawl. The demon's midnight blue hair undulated around her head in the night wind; her leathery black wings stroked the air slowly.

As the demon aimed at me, a voice rose from the depths of my mind—something uncannily familiar. *I am not the weak mortal you think I am.*

Dark power surged from the ground up, from the train tracks, into the stilts, into the floor beneath my feet. *My* power. A strange, primal music swelled in me. The life buried beneath the stones of this city was singing, and I could harness its energy. I called to the tree roots and the spirits of the dead under the soil.

The trees fed off the earth that was once my home. I could call the poplar tree. My child.

Down by the river, the Tower of Bones
If you're lost, Dovren is home.

My eyes went wide, and my body ignited with power. As it did, I called to the tree.

A sharp poplar branch shot up from the ground and impaled the demon through her chest, right through where her heart would be.

She slumped forward, dropping the bow and arrow. As I stared, her body turned dark gray, and cracks opened in her skin. She desiccated, then turned into dust that floated away on the night wind. Only the tree remained.

I looked down at myself, at how she'd pinned me to the wall.

I understood why they wanted Samael. But why me? Maybe Alice wasn't finished with me.

I started tearing at my dress, ripping it to free myself. Then, I whirled to look out the broken windows. A handful of dead demons lay on the ground.

I sucked in a deep breath, my body trembling. Samael flew above the grassy, moonlit park. Arrows protruded from his body. His flight was jagged now, and he looked like he was struggling to stay in the air.

Only one demon remained, nocking her final arrow. But before she could unleash it, Samael swooped forward and slashed his blade through her throat. Her body—and head—fell to the ground.

I loosed a long breath and turned to the doorway. The spiked poplar branch still jutted into the sky before me.

Pain burned on my wrist, and when I looked down, a silver tattoo gleamed on my skin—a crescent moon with thorny vines wrapped around it. Then, as quickly as it had arrived, the tattoo disappeared. I gaped at where it had been.

I'd seen that exact symbol in the locked room.

Was this the ghost's power?

16

SAMAEL

Pain shot through my wings and shoulder where the demons' arrows had pierced me, and I was no longer flying straight. But still—I had to cut out the demons' hearts before they would be truly dead. It was the only way to make sure they wouldn't come soaring after me again in a few minutes.

I careened toward the earth, where my enemies lay twitching. I could capture one of these demons, but it would do no good. Soulless down to her marrow, she'd be impervious to pain, to threats. She'd never give up information.

Gritting my teeth, I landed hard on the earth, stumbling. The pain of an injured wing was indescribable. It was the sort of pain that robbed you of thought, that narrowed the world down entirely to agony in the one spot where it was wounded. It wasn't just a physical pain, but a disturbing sense of being fundamentally broken.

From the gathered shadows, a demon lurched up from the ground, her severed body already healing. She let out a blood-curdling shriek, and I pivoted to see her aiming another arrow at me. Her hair streamed behind her, sleek and blue. Her eyes were pools of darkness—empty, gleaming.

Death was the only way to deal with a demon.

She let the arrow fly. Gritting my teeth, I managed to deflect it with my sword, but she was already nocking another. Nearby, another demon started to rise from the dirt. The pure thrill of battle vibrated down my limbs, skimming my wings until they no longer hurt. I lunged for the demons, losing myself in the glory of war.

With each demon I killed, I was able to forget, just a little more, that one word knelling in my brain. *Mediocre*.

Why did I care so much what the mortal woman thought? It was absurd.

I didn't care what anyone thought of me.

Asmodai split through the demon's bow, then I brought it back around through her neck.

Ordinary. I was nothing of the sort.

I arced around sharply, swooping to attack another demon. With each strike of my sword, I began to push the word *mediocre* further into the depths of my thoughts, until it no longer had meaning. Until, at last, there was nothing left but the dark beauty of death, and I felt like a god again.

I began to cut out the demons' hearts.

No pain, no doubts, only a distant memory of that little mortal in the house above the tracks.

My thoughts dimmed as I worked, the dust of their desiccated bodies floating on the wind. Only when I destroyed a demon's heart would her body turn to dust, destroying her for good. My mind flickered with long-forgotten memories—my life before the fall, my sword gleaming with blood. Light all around me.

I knelt over the body of a demon, staring into her dark eyes. As my blade carved out her heart, she turned to ash beneath me.

But out of the corner of my eye, I glimpsed movement. Another demon was rising from the ground, wings spread out behind her.

Except she wasn't flying toward me. She was flying for Lila.

My blood pounded hard, and I gripped Asmodai.

I hardly felt any pain at all as I rushed toward Lila.

17

LILA

Another demon swept into the shack. Her head was bent at an odd angle, blood dripping from a deep gash in her neck. Her mouth was strained into an unnatural grimace.

My fingers twitched, ready to call forth another tree branch. When the demon raised her bow, I felt the power moving up from my feet into my thighs again. Earthy magic filled me.

But before I could strike, I felt another dark force moving closer—Samael. He appeared behind her, wings spread out against the night sky, and his sword pierced her back, protruding from her chest. For a moment, she hung limp. Then, she crumbled into dust.

Samael sheathed his sword, and his wings disappeared as he reached the doorway. Celestial fire blazed in his eyes. My gaze trailed down his body, and I winced at what I saw—he was still riddled with broken arrow shafts.

Sucking in a breath, I opened his cloak. He'd already snapped off and pulled some of the arrows from his flesh, but fragments of wood still pierced him, and blood poured from the wounds.

"Are you okay?" I asked. "We need to get those arrows out of you."

But he didn't seem to notice or care about his own injuries. His voice was a sharp blade as he said, "Which of the Fallen taught you magic?"

"None of them." I looked up at his face, frowning. Shimmering gold shone from his cheekbones and flaming chains encircled his enormous chest. This was Samael shifting into his purest form: sublime and dreadful.

And very, very interested in me. His gaze swept down my bare legs, where I'd ripped the hem of my skirt.

"I don't believe you." He took a step closer and pressed his palms against the wood on either side of my head. "If no one taught you, then how do you know magic? You're not a demon. You're not a nephilim. Someone taught you."

My breath quickened. "Nope."

"You little liar." His voice had taken on a velvety tone. "How is it possible for you to have this magic at your fingertips and not know?"

"Why don't you tell me why you're all weird about that room you keep locked up?"

"No."

"I guess we're at another impasse." I didn't have any idea where my magic came from. It unnerved me, because the magic itself felt dark. What if I had my own evil magic buried inside me? What would I be like when it came out?

I shivered, wondering if demons could have children. If I were half-demon, would Samael want me dead like the others?

I bit my lip. "I don't know that the magic even came from me. It probably came from one of the other demons. But we can ponder this mystery later. If those demons found us here, more could find us. I don't want to find out what the Free Men have in store for us."

But he wasn't moving. His gaze was searing me, taking me apart like he was penetrating my very soul. Then, his eyes roved down my body once more, and he moved his hand to my waist.

"I don't think you're telling me the truth," he murmured, his voice sliding into a seductive tone. He lowered his face to mine, breath warming the side of my face. "How do I make you more honest?"

My pulse raced as I felt the heat pouring off his body, and the dark thrum of his magic. "You could start by admitting the truth yourself. You find me more interesting than any other woman strutting around half naked."

"You first," he whispered.

But he didn't give me a chance to answer, sliding his lips over mine. For just a moment, the kiss seemed tentative, like he had no idea what was happening. He kissed me as if he were testing out something dangerous. But even this light brush of his lips against mine made me melt into him, my knees going weak. Pleasure vibrated through my body, and his fingers flexed hard on my waist.

But he was holding back. It wasn't enough. Any touch from an angel was dangerous. An angel's kiss was fuel to a sexual flame that, once lit, could never be put out. His magic skimmed over my body, stroking me with heat. Ecstasy rippled through me, and I arched into him, wrapping my arms tight around his neck.

As my pulse started to race out of control, his lips parted against mine. The kiss became more intense, slow and possessive. He was growing hungrier, his desire deeper and more dangerous, tongue sweeping against mine. I wrapped my legs around him, and he lifted me up, pressing me against the wall.

As his hands swept under my bum, an aching heat built in my core.

Then, with a nip to my lower lip, he pulled away from the kiss.

He had kissed me. Victorious, I arched an eyebrow at him.

As if he knew what I was thinking, he said, "It was the ripped dress and my primal state."

Anger flared. "Of course. Showing off my wares again. And just so you know, I kissed you back out of sheer loneliness and desperation, my most ordinary and banal companion."

He winced, and for a moment, I thought it was because of my stinging retort. Then, I saw him touch his chest where one of the arrows had pierced him.

"You feel it now, don't you? The arrows weren't hurting you before, but now I can see it. How many times were you hit?"

"Six," he said huskily. "My wing will take a while to heal. I think I can still fly, though. I can get us back."

"Hang on." I opened his cloak again. "Just let me pull some of the broken arrows from you."

I winced at the fragments of wood and the blood pouring from him. Carefully, I began to pull wood splinters from one of the wounds in his chest, using my fingertips. He inhaled sharply.

"How did the demons find us?" I asked, hoping to distract him.

All his muscles had gone completely tense, which was making this harder. "They were trackers. They hunt by scent."

"Did any of them make it away?"

"No, which means they can't report back to the Free Men that we were here." He grimaced, covering the wound in his abdomen. "That's enough, Lila. Thank you. Emma has tools at home she can use."

Brooking no argument, Samael swept me up into his arms, pulling me against his chest. As he took to the air, my mind kept jolting back to the feel of that magic I'd used.

I wanted to see Mum. I wanted to ask her if she could tell me more about what I was. Her story was that I'd arrived in a basket on her doorstep. But that wasn't a very likely story, was it? I wanted to know the truth.

I wrapped my arms around Samael's neck as he flew, the wind whipping over us. "Samael. I want to see my mum tomorrow."

"No."

"Why not?"

"Because she could be working for the Free Men."

I snorted. "She's not working for the Free Men. She could hardly get out of bed. She'd be a fucking liability."

"Your sister works for the Free Men. And what if your mother is no longer a drunk?"

"She's not political."

"My answer is no."

I clenched my jaw, irritation simmering. I *hated* being controlled. "Arsehole."

Whether Samael approved or not, I would get to her.

I just needed to find my way out.

18

LILA

In my dark room once more, I stared out the window at the murky moat below. I was trying to forget the earth-shattering kiss with Samael. I was pretty sure he had forgotten it, which irritated me beyond belief.

It was the ripped dress and my primal state.

Tosser.

At least it seemed cozy in here, no ghosts on the horizon. From now on, in this room, I'd be keeping the lantern on at all times. Ghosts didn't come when the lights were on. *Everyone* knew that. On another positive note, my belly was full from the late dinner after we returned—roasted chicken, potatoes, parsnips, and wine. Another delicious dinner eaten alone.

I still wore the ripped black dress, I realized as I looked down at my bare legs. Sorry, my *wares*. I supposed I'd avoided changing so far because the last time I'd taken my clothes off, the ghost thought it was a perfect time to attack. Wrestling naked on the bathroom floor felt deeply undignified.

I looked out at the thorny garden and the ruined gate. I

wanted to find Mum in the priory, but I'd need to figure out how to make that happen.

As I stared out the window, Jenny Squawks swept past, and for a moment I thought she was going to land on the windowsill. Instead, she turned sharply for the river, then started squawking again, frantically flapping her wings.

I frowned. I watched her do it again, frantically circling toward the river, then squawking manically, her flight erratic.

Something was wrong with her.

In fact, it almost looked as if she couldn't make it past the moat. That was exactly where the pain had gripped me when I'd tried to leave.

Was this magic curse working on Jenny also? But I'd seen others come and go from the castle—Oswald, Emma, some of the cooks.

What did Jenny and I have in common?

I turned, looking back at the remains of my dinner, and my gaze sharpened on the fruit, a beautiful garnet red and full of seeds. I'd been feeding her that fruit ...

I'd never actually seen her fly over the moat since I'd fed it to her.

Perhaps it was enchanted. It was odd, after all, that they gave it to me every night. The rest of the food changed—but not the fruit.

Pulling open the window, I called to Jenny. She swooped inside, her feathers ruffled, looking upset.

I pet her head. "I'm sorry, little bird. We have been poisoned by an evil angel."

I leaned out the window, peering down at the moat and the bridge that spanned it. Under the moonlight, the water had a dark, ominous sheen. This place was supposed to be protected by angelic charms, and yet I had the strangest premonition that something terrible would happen in that

RAPTURE

moat. Maybe it was the way the ghost had tormented me—the water and leaves. I shivered and closed the window again.

The wind whistled through a tiny crack in the window, unsettling me. Still, I was so exhausted my eyes were drifting closed. But I didn't want to sleep. If I let my guard down, the ghost would return.

I took a deep breath, glancing out the window again. Maybe it wasn't that something terrible would happen here in the future. Maybe it already had.

After all, Samael kept that room locked for a reason. Maybe he'd been the one to lock up the Iron Queen.

I pressed my palms against the cool glass. As I did, a voice whispered, *You know what you are, Lila.*

I breathed slowly, in and out, gritting my teeth. "No, I have no idea, actually. Do you want to fill me in?" My voice came out sharp and angry.

You are evil, the voice replied.

Dread slithered over my skin, and I looked down at my wrist. There, the silver tattoo gleamed again—the crescent moon wrapped in thorny vines. Symbols of life, of night. Was the person who had lived in that room connected to me, or was I simply drawing from her power here?

Then, a cold draft rippled over the room, and the lantern snuffed out, cloaking the room in darkness.

Oh, bollocks. Frantic, I turned the lantern on again, bringing the flame up high.

From nowhere, an icy wind rushed past, smothering the flame again.

She was coming for me.

I reached for the acorn at my neck—the thing that would keep me safe—but it wasn't there. The little bit of string must have snapped during the battle with the demons, or perhaps somewhere in this room.

I whirled, trying to see in the dark. Where had the acorn gone?

Maybe I should get out of here. I could find Emma or Oswald. The ghost wouldn't appear around others; she wanted me to seem like a bloody lunatic. That was all part of the fun for her, wasn't it?

I turned, passing the mirror. But as I did, something stopped me dead in my tracks. Entranced, I could no longer move forward. I wanted to look in the mirror. It called to me like a siren.

Slowly, I turned my head, and my breath caught in my throat. In the reflection, my hair wafted around my head, undulating above me like I was underwater. My eyes had darkened to a pure, void black, and my arms lifted, wrists raising in the air before me. In the center of my forehead, the silver symbol blazed—a moon with vines.

I'll leave you alone when you admit what you are. Evil. Corrupted.

Her words took root in my mind, like an invasive species crawling over the inside of my skull. Ivy would make its home in my thoughts, taking over.

You were meant to be alone. To die alone. There is power in isolation.

A brutal ache gnawed at my chest.

He won't love you. And when he learns what you are, he will kill you. Might as well get there first.

At last, I managed to break free. Panic clawed at my chest as I ran for the door. But before I could get to it, an invisible force slammed into me, knocking me to the ground. I tried to scramble to my knees, but my throat was filling with water again. Foul, filthy liquid slid down my gullet, and I couldn't get any air.

This was how it would all end, choking to death alone.

I couldn't scream. My body thrashed, spasming, limbs

knocking into the furniture. The weight of silty water pressed down on me. It was the moat, wasn't it? I was drowning in the moat.

This had happened before ...

My vision started to go dark. Then, it filled with a terrifying image—Samael's true face, his eyes blazing with primordial fire. This wasn't Samael anymore. This was the reaper, and his gaze held no mercy, no love.

He reached for me, his fist plunging into my ribcage, snapping bones. Then I was falling, plummeting through the icy air. Thrown from the window. I slammed into the surface of the moat. The murky depths filled my lungs, and I felt my life leaving me as my arms floated up above my head ...

Desperate, I reached out, scrambling for anything around me. My fingers grasped something round and hard. It was salvation somehow, and I pulled it to my chest, gasping for air. The illusion of the moat disappeared again. The reaper was gone.

I was lying on the floor of the bedroom, my breath labored, rasping. The lantern was lit once again, warm light dancing over the room. I brought the little acorn before my eyes, relieved to have found it.

When I looked down at myself, I found red marks on my arms and legs where I'd been slamming them into the furniture. Soon, they'd form into purple bruises. I touched my cheekbone, feeling a welt forming there already.

But not everything had disappeared. Dirty water still filled my mouth, and I rolled over onto my hands and knees, coughing up some of the moat onto the floor.

That theory about how ghosts couldn't actually hurt you? That was wrong.

I had the strange sense that she was jealous of me. She wanted me to know Samael didn't love me. Was she a past lover of his? I knew only that he'd never had sex with a mortal woman. But a demon? Maybe he had.

Still on the floor, I hugged myself. Shivering, I leaned against the bed, clutching the acorn hard in my fist. I wasn't sure how much time had passed when my breathing started to slow.

A knock sounded at my door, and I nearly jumped out of my skin.

I clutched the acorn in my sweaty palm. "Who's there?" My voice came out sounding furious.

I pulled open the door to find *him* standing with his cowl raised over his head, face enshrouded.

"Yes?" My voice shook.

"What happened to you?"

I looked down at my body, where the bruises were already starting to turn purple. The thing was, he'd never believe me if I told him it was the ghost. He'd already said as much.

"Nothing," I said sharply. I held the acorn out to him. "But can you ask Oswald to send up more of these?"

Every now and then, you see yourself from a distance, how you must look to others. And at that moment, I realized how completely and utterly mad I must look—my hair wild, holding out an acorn and asking for more of them.

"Why do you want an acorn, and what happened to you?"

I closed my fingers around the acorn. "It's just good luck. What do you want?"

Samael raised one of his arms, leaning against the door frame. "I sensed something was wrong. And now I can see that it is."

My mind ignited with a picture of how he'd looked in the vision—merciless. Ruthless. "Well, I'm locked in this castle by a death angel, so I guess something is kind of wrong. How close are you to becoming the reaper?"

"What are the bruises from?"

"The ghost." He wouldn't believe me.

"Right." He arched an eyebrow. "Why are you asking about the reaper?"

"I'm just thinking about your warning, that's all. About how you're dangerous. Maybe I'd like to know more about this reaper side of you."

He pulled his gaze away from me, staring into the hall. "Sourial would probably be delighted to give you the history. I slaughtered people up and down Albia, Clovia, the islands. I don't remember most of it. Just little flashes. Blood mixing with the dirt to become red mud. Sometimes I hear the screams." When he looked at me again, his eyes glinted with confusion. "You seem different, suddenly. And you still aren't telling me the truth."

My jaw tightened. "You won't hear the truth. And the truth is, I want to see my Mum. I don't know where my magic comes from, and I'd like to find out. She might know more than she has let on. But I don't want you listening in."

He frowned. "As my prisoner, you're not in a position to make demands."

Actually, I was, considering I now knew how to escape. But I'd keep that part to myself. I cocked my hip. "You need me to participate in this wedding, don't you? And you want it to look real."

His expression darkened. "Are you threatening me?"

"Absolutely."

A muscle twitched in his jaw. "Fine."

The air seemed too thin, growing colder as the silence stretched out.

Looks like I hit my mark.

I smiled. "Great! I knew we could work something out."

His brow furrowed as he took in the blooming bruises on my arms and legs. Then, he traced a fingertip very gently over the bruise on my cheek. "What happened to you?" he asked again.

"Can you confirm about tomorrow?" I pressed. "We have a deal, right?"

He pulled his hand away. "I'll take you to her tomorrow. Now tell me what happened."

I gripped the acorn like a lifeline, nodding. "I don't suppose you'd believe me if I said it was a ghost."

Torchlight and shadows danced back and forth over the hall where Samael stood, and he went very still. A cool draft whipped past me, toying with my hair. Instead of answering, he simply walked away, and the door closed behind him, leaving me alone.

Still gripping my acorn, I crossed to the lantern and turned it up. I wanted to know more about demons, more about the reaper. More about ghosts.

Knowledge was power, and I had an arsenal of books at my fingertips. I'd arm myself to the teeth, so when my little phantom friend returned, I'd at least have a better idea of how to fight her.

Just as I was crossing to the shelves, another knock sounded on my door.

This time, I opened the door to see Emma, a candle and taper in her hands. She frowned at my arms. "Are you all right? Samael said there was something wrong with you."

"A ghost attacked me." I opened the door wider. "Do you have any interest in helping me read about ghosts?"

"Excuse me?"

"I can read the books a little bit, but with your help, it will go faster. I want to find out about the types of ghosts that can beat the ever-loving shit out of you, because that is what happened to me this evening. I even coughed up moat water—" I pointed at the floor, where I'd vomited up a bit of the moat, but by now, the stones were completely dry.

Bloody hell.

"I just want to learn more about ghosts," I said a little more uncertainly.

She narrowed her eyes, tilting her head. "Okay."

Desperation pierced me. "I didn't do this to myself, Emma."

Her forehead crinkled. "Fine. Well, at least this will be amusing. I'll see if I can find any ghost books."

"Good. Because there's something evil in this castle."

Besides Samael.

19

LILA

By the time Emma left, I had no new information. I had, however, managed to find an account of the reaper from five centuries ago, complete with pictures of villages full of dead people and blood running through the streets. The accounts left me feeling cold and slightly terrified.

But even with Emma's help, I found nothing about ghosts.

I supposed the chances of finding a book called *Why a Manifestation of Evil is Attacking you with Leaves* were not particularly high.

It must have been three o'clock by the time I was lying in bed with the lights out. I closed my eyes, willing sleep to come. With the acorn clenched tightly in my fist, I wasn't as worried about the ghost.

But something else kept creeping into my mind. It was the memory of that kiss earlier. The possessive feeling of his hand on my body. The way he'd pinned me to the wall. The dark, molten heat of his mouth, his tongue sweeping against mine. I should have been remembering what he kept saying—

that I was about as interesting as any other half-naked woman. But his kiss told a different story.

As I lay in bed, staring at the ceiling, the kiss replayed in my mind, again and again. I wanted to feel his mouth on me, exploring.

Sighing, I rolled over. My body was growing hot, and I threw off the sheets. Every time I closed my eyes again, it was like I could feel his magic skimming over my skin, making me ache for him.

Why was it so bloody hot in here? I pulled my nightgown up higher.

A crack of light illuminated the room as the door opened, and I gasped.

I sat upright, staring at Samael. With my cheeks heating, I tugged down my nightgown again. "What are you doing in here?"

He crossed to the edge of my bed and sat. I watched his searing gaze moving up and down my bare legs. One of his hands was pressed to the mattress close to my thigh, the point of contact making my skin flush. Moonlight poured through the window, lighting the room enough for me to make out that he wasn't wearing a cloak but a black shirt that sculpted his muscles. Hard not to stare.

"I want to know who taught you magic," he said quietly. "You killed that demon, but I don't know how. I can see that you're mortal. I can feel it and smell it."

I held his gaze. "I'm an ordinary mortal. Just a run of the mill, workaday human with ordinary *wares*."

"But you're keeping secrets from me." His dominating tone made my pulse race faster. His seductive magic simmered up my legs in a way that made my knees tremble.

I shrugged. "All I know, Samael, is that if you're here in my room in the middle of the night, I must be occupying your thoughts an awful lot."

He leaned forward, planting his hands on either side of my hips. The feel of his wrists through the silk of the nightgown was setting me on fire. His eyes smoldered.

Then, he whispered in my ear, "Don't play games with me, mortal. You will not win."

I shuddered at the threat, a forbidden pleasure rippling over me. Something dark and dangerous was coursing through me now, and I found I very much wanted to play games with him.

With every deep breath I took, the silky material of my nightgown was brushing gently up and down over my nipples. I wanted his mouth to replace the material. I felt my body straining against the nightgown, and I thought of ripping it off. Liquid heat pooled at the apex of my thighs.

For a moment, I tried to remind myself how arrogant he was, and that we were locked in a battle of wills. But the thought evaporated like water on hot stone.

I licked my lips. "Are you sure I wouldn't win?"

"You know what I think? I think you need some lessons in honesty."

My heart fluttered as he rose from the bed and ripped the thin, silky banner off the wall. Gripping it at the top, he tore it in two. I wasn't sure exactly what he was doing, but anticipation was making my pulse race anyway.

He climbed on the bed, then dragged my pillows into the center of the mattress.

"What are you doing?" I asked, giving him a defiant look.

He turned to me, planting his hands firmly on either side of my hips again. The look he was giving me was dark, molten. The heat of his magic kissed my skin, making my breath come faster. He *was* winning this battle of wills; any moment now, I'd be doing whatever he wanted.

"I'm going to get answers out of you." He slid his hands under my bum and lifted me up, then positioned me face down, hips over the pillows, arse in the air. "An interrogation."

"Is this how you torture all your captives?"

"Not at all. But you can keep your mouth closed until you're ready to tell me where you learned magic."

As my head rested on the bed, I felt him tying my wrists together behind my back. I *should* protest, and yet maybe this wasn't the worst way to be interrogated.

Samael moved behind me, one knee on either side of my thighs. He reached for the straps of my nightgown, pulling them down until the neckline was below my breasts. Cool castle air hit my back, and I ached to feel his hands on me. My nipples hardened to sensitive points.

With an excruciatingly light stroke, he brushed his fingertips over my ribs, beneath my breasts—slow, light circles, scorching. Each stroke of his fingertips was torture, his addictive touch was making my breasts feel fuller, hypersensitive, even though he wasn't touching them. As I arched my back, my breasts grazed against the silk sheets, up and down, my nipples aching to be touched. I turned my head against the mattress.

"You want to know how I learned magic?" I said breathlessly. "I didn't."

"Where does the magic come from?"

"From the earth, I think."

"Good. There's some truth at last." His thumbs brushed over my hypersensitive nipples. My toes curled, body clenching with need, and I gasped.

He leaned down over me, hands on either side of my head. He'd taken off his shirt, and his bare chest pressed against my back, warming my bare shoulders. The ache between my legs was so intense I could think of nothing but him filling me.

"You want more of me, don't you?"

"Yes," I whispered.

With a sharp tug, he yanked the hem of my nightgown up, and the air kissed my bare thighs. I was helpless before him, my hips thrust up toward him.

"Then tell me what you are." He traced a single fingertip down my spine, leaving incinerating heat in its wake. I wanted him to stroke every inch of my body, but I didn't have the answers he was looking for.

"I don't know."

With a slow, lazy touch, he ran a finger down to the edge of my underwear. His fingertips swept around, tracing around my waist to the hollow of my hips. My body buzzed for him, electrified.

"I don't know," I said again. I just wanted him inside me.

But he was drawing this out. His hand skimmed back around my hip, around my thigh. He traced slowly up and down my inner thigh with the back of his knuckles.

God, I needed more contact. I felt my legs widening. My breath came faster, pulse racing. I needed to feel him between my legs.

He was moving higher, but it was deliberately slow. He was trying to drive me insane.

"Samael," I whispered.

"You'll get what you need only when you give me what I need. What are you?"

At last, he grazed his fingertips gently over the silk between my legs. A low, trembling moan escaped my lips. I was slick with desire for him. To my frustration, he kept his touch excruciatingly soft, torturing me. As he stroked the silk between my legs, my nipples continued to brush against the sheets beneath me. My body was shaking in desperation for him, hips moving against him for more contact. He pulled his hand away again.

One hand gripped my hair, holding me right where he

wanted me. The other was tracing lightly, tormenting me. At last, he pulled down my underwear—one inch at a time.

Panting, I cried out his name.

※

My eyes snapped open, and I found myself alone, catching my breath. One of my hands was in my underwear, and I'd been sleeping on top of the covers. Morning light streamed in through the window. Disoriented, I sat up and looked around my room. The banner was still hanging on the wall, in one piece. Disappointment pierced me.

I pulled my hand away. No, it was good that it was just a dream. Samael, after all, wasn't willing to admit that he liked me.

That arrogant angel bastard had *really* gotten in my head, which was deeply annoying. And concerning. I wondered if the more I kissed him, the more addicted I'd become to his touch.

If I was going to get by in the dangerous world of the Fallen, I couldn't lose myself to sexual obsessions.

Flinging my legs over the side of the bed, I stood to head for the bathroom. I'd be taking a *very* cold bath before I met with Samael again this morning.

And then, I'd try to find out exactly what the fuck I was.

20

LILA

One breakfast and two cold baths later, I was walking with Samael outside. Even after the ice water, I could not bloody stop thinking about that dream. Three times he'd caught me staring at him, and each time, my face would burn furiously.

But I'd keep this secret well hidden.

As we walked, my mind was dazed, foggy. Completely sleep deprived. The cold wind bit at my skin, but the sun shone brightly today. I pulled my cloak tight.

The good news was that the fatigue was dulling my fluttering nerves over the upcoming conversation with Mum. Telling her that her natural-born daughter had faked her own death and joined a murder cult was not something I'd particularly enjoy. Especially considering Mum was newly sober now, and wouldn't drift off in a gin haze. The horror of it all would be sharp.

As we walked through the sun-drenched streets toward the priory, Samael cut me a sharp look. "Why do you keep looking at me like that?"

My cheeks flamed, but I schooled my features. "Looking at you like what?"

"With so much intensity. What sort of schemes and machinations do you have in mind now? You're always plotting something, aren't you?"

Oh, nothing. Just schemes involving silk restraints and your hands on me.

I cleared my throat. "You told me you're dangerous. Just keeping my eye on you in case you snap and try to kill me."

"How do you envision that fight playing out, should it come down to it?"

"Perhaps I'd summon a tree branch to strangle you."

He stopped abruptly, turning to me. "How? This particular type of magic ..." He trailed off. Something really unnerved him about this.

"What?" I asked.

He shook his head. "It reminds me of something I'd rather forget."

"Are you going to tell me what that is, or will I have to tie you up and torture it out of you?"

He narrowed his eyes. "What are you talking about?"

"There's something dark in your castle. An evil presence. A tragedy, maybe. Did you know that there's an old legend? A king loved a woman so much, he trapped her in the Iron Fortress. While she was locked up, she lost her mind."

Shadows darkened his eyes. "I'm not an expert in love, but I don't think that's how it works."

Frustration tightened my chest. Why couldn't he just tell me the truth? "And that wasn't what happened, was it?" I pressed. "It wasn't a king. It was you. *You* were the first one to live in the castle. A woman lived in that room you keep locked. And you haven't changed her room since. She meant something to you."

"It wasn't love," his quiet voice held a sharp edge—a warning, almost.

"So why have you kept her room like it is?"

"To remind myself of what evil feels like, and how I should never again let down my guard."

I felt my blood growing colder. "Was she a demon?"

A lick of flames lit up his eyes. "Yes. And I should have killed her as soon as I met her."

Fear slid over my skin. "Why?"

"A demon can't love. They can only pretend, feign love. A demon will twist your mind and your heart and try to suck the life from you so they can feel. And I made the mistake of agreeing to marry her. She was dangerous and traitorous. But we're almost to the priory, and I've told you more than you need to know already. All that was centuries ago. It doesn't have anything to do with anything."

I felt a bizarre twinge of jealousy that he'd been married before. No *wonder* the ghost seemed threatened by me. I'd sensed her envy, too.

We turned into Sanguine Square, where the kings had once burned traitors and heretics. Today, it was where the butchers sold their meat; the sun shone over market stalls, and the air stank of blood. The Priory of the Holy Sisters stood just across the way.

At last, we arrived at the gleaming white gatehouse of the priory—an old timber frame structure above a stone entrance. Samael pushed through the door and strode onto the stone path.

I hugged myself, steeling my nerves for the conversation that was about to unfold.

As I crossed through the old gatehouse, I took in the archaic beauty of the place. A gothic building of dark stone rose before us, and a courtyard spread out to our right, encircled by arched walkways. A couple of Holy Sisters walked past a fountain, hands folded, expressions somber.

On the left was a cemetery, with crooked grave markers jutting from the soil like bony fingers of stone. In the old days, people thought you had to be buried in a priory cemetery, or you wouldn't get to Heaven. So, they'd stacked the bodies on top of each other, forming mounds of the dead under the earth. It was apparently the only way to ensure a luxurious afterlife.

But as a high-pitched keening sound wended through the air, I realized with a rising sense of dread that I would not be talking to Sober Mum at all today. Sober Mum was not here. Because the person singing the Albian folksong about a courtesan named Lucy was most definitely Drunk Mum. The song was one of her favorites after a bottle of gin.

Frustration sparked. The entire point of paying for this place had been to get her off the gin. Sighing deeply, I pointed to one of the archways on the other side of the courtyard. "I hear her over there."

"That noise?" Samael's footfalls echoed off the flagstones as we crossed into one of the arched corridors. "That noise is your mother?"

"Ever since Alice left, it's how she drowns her sadness." My chest felt empty, hollow. "I used to blame you for that. Everyone thought you killed Alice. Now I have Alice to blame."

Confusion glinted in his eyes, and an intense curiosity. "Having a family seems complicated. Is it worth it?"

Good question. "Yes," I said at last. "Without them I'd feel very alone. You have no family at all?"

"No. I was created, not born."

When we rounded a corner, I found her in a hall with open arches. A door was open nearby, giving a view of a messy room with an unmade bed, which I presumed was hers.

Eyes closed, she sat slumped on a wooden bench against the wall, looking the same as ever. The same red blooms of gin blossoms spread over her nose. Her hair was a tangle of knots. A chunk of bread lay in her hand as she dozed, and pigeons stared up at her, hoping for some of the crumbs that littered her skirt. The only thing noticeably different was the long, white frock. At least she looked clean.

The cold winter wind toyed with her skirts and tangled hair. She clutched a bottle of gin, and her breath made clouds in front of her face.

I sat next to her on the bench and touched her arm. She snorted a bit, but kept her eyes closed.

"Mum." I squeezed her arm harder.

Her eyes snapped open, and she yelped, nearly dropping her gin as she jolted awake. Dazed, her gaze slowly drifted to me. A smile warmed her face, and her expression softened. "There you are. My girl. You were always my favorite one."

I smiled back at her. "I was?"

She blinked. "Oh. I thought you were Alice for a second."

The breath left my lungs, and I felt my eyes sting. "No, just me."

She looked startled, flustered. "You were my favorite also, Lila. I loved you both. A mum can have more than one favorite."

"If Alice were here, would you stop drinking all the gin?"

She frowned at me. "They tried taking my medicine away, but I get sick without it. I would shake and rave. They understand, now, that it helps me."

"You need less medicine. You need a little less every day."

She brightened. "You came to pay me a visit," she said happily. "I missed you."

I took a deep breath. "There's something you need to know. I don't want you to get too excited, Mum, because she's turned into something very different. But she's alive."

She grabbed my arm, joy spreading over her features. "Alice?"

God, I had to get this out quickly before she got too excited. "Yes, but she's part of a murderous cult. They kill people."

She blinked at me. "That doesn't sound right. Murderous?"

"It's not right, Mum, but it's happening. They're Albian nationalists who want to kill everyone they think doesn't belong. She's part of it, and so is Finn."

The pigeons cooed at Mum's feet, pecking at the crumbs. "Not Finn! You're not going to do anything bad to her, are you?"

"Why do you think I would do something bad to her?"

She cocked her head. "Because of what you are, Lila."

My heart started to pound, and I grabbed her arm. She *did* know more than she let on. I stole a quick glance behind me at Samael, making sure he was out of earshot. He lingered in the archway, too far away to overhear. Just as I'd asked, he was giving us privacy.

Turning back, I whispered, "What am I, Mum?"

She lifted a finger to her lips, giggling. "Shhhhhhh. Secret, isn't it? Always so many secrets. And thing is about secrets ... they press down on your chest and crush you after a while, don't they? Because when you have secrets, you're totally alone. It's just you and your secrets, and they bury you alive."

"Then tell, Mum. It's important, and you'll feel better. You'll feel less alone. Less buried."

"You have secrets, too, don't you?" Her gaze flicked behind me to where Samael stood. "Who's this?"

Oh, just my fiancée, the Angel of Death. "Don't worry about him, Mum. I want to know who I am. Where I came from."

She took a sip of her flask, then brought a hand to her

mouth, laughing. "Well, I couldn't tell people the truth, could I? It wasn't natural. Thought they might kill you."

My pulse was racing faster now, my grip tightening on her arm. "What wasn't?"

"I said I found you on the doorstep. But that wasn't the truth. Because what happened was ..." Her eyes drifted to the left, in a daze. "I was walking home with Alice, past the Priory of Thorns. And you know the courtyard of ruins? Where the pink tea roses climb over the stones. That was where I found you, crying in a forgotten corner."

I stared at her. This was not the story she'd told me long ago. "Someone left me in a basket in the ruins."

"Not a basket, no. That would have been more normal. It was the strangest thing ... you were covered in dirt, my love. And I thought I saw you crawl *from* the dirt. Like you rose from the ground itself. You clawed your way out. You rose from the earth."

My jaw dropped. "What are you talking about?"

"You climbed from the soil. Just a little baby, but strong enough to work your way out of the earth. Like a mushroom growing. Very unnatural. But whatever you were, I couldn't leave you there, could I? Whatever you were, you were hungry. You were always so hungry. You'd scream and scream all night for milk."

Horror slid through my bones. "Someone buried me?"

Mum shrugged. "I didn't know. I think that must have happened, but I had the strangest sense ... it seemed like you grew there, maybe, like a flower." She shook her head. "I know it doesn't make sense. I was still nursing Alice then. What was the harm? I could feed you. It wasn't easy, mind you," she added with a weak laugh. "You wanted so much milk. I thought you'd leave me a dried husk. But I couldn't leave a baby in the dirt. I wanted to keep you safe. And I knew you weren't normal. When you were a baby, your eyes were black as the night ..."

My stomach plummeted. "What?"

"I was so relieved when they turned normal again. Because I knew ... I knew something was wrong. Something was a bit off. But I loved you anyway. I'd only let people see you when you were asleep, so they couldn't see your black eyes."

My mouth had gone dry. What the *fuck?* I wasn't a soulless demon. I didn't have tangible proof that I had a soul, but clearly, I bloody had one. I felt things. I loved people.

I swallowed hard. "Does Alice know?"

Mum's eyes were glazed, but she nodded. "It was crushing me, the secret. Like I said, secrets make you feel alone. She kept asking where you came from. And we were always so close. So I told her one day. But it upset her. And then she was just gone."

Something twisted in my chest. The words of the ghost were still climbing around inside my mind. *Admit what you are.*

"There's nothing wrong with me, Mum," I said defensively, but I didn't believe it anymore. "Wherever I came from, I'm not evil."

She didn't seem to hear me. Her eyes were unfocused again. "I always knew. My two girls, so different but so alike. One light, one dark. One good, and one evil. But I loved you both anyway."

"I'm not evil," I said in a harsh whisper.

The ghost's words snaking around inside my skull, invasive vines. *You were meant to be alone.*

"Shut up," I whispered.

Mum's eyes were closing again; she was no longer listening. She slumped over on the bench, head on the cold stone.

Tears stung my eyes. I stood, my heart hammering, and

turned back to Samael. I rushed over to him, desperate to be away from here.

When I reached him, he touched my arm. "What did she say?"

I blinked, trying to clear the tears from my eyes. There was, of course, the possibility that she was just drunk off her arse. "That Alice was her favorite. And she's just drunk. Nothing important. It didn't make a lot of sense. I'm going to have a word with the Holy Sisters about cutting down her gin."

His gaze went to Mum. His jaw clenched, and he stalked past me. I started to grab his arm, but he moved too swiftly. Was he going to interrogate her himself? "Samael!"

But he kept walking right past her, into her room. A moment later, he came out with a blanket. He covered her in the blanket, tucking it around her to keep her warm. Then he stared at her, looking perplexed.

He plucked her bottle of gin from her arm and dumped it out onto the stone.

When it was done, he crossed back to me, his brow furrowed. "I'll speak to the Holy Sisters."

I stood in shock, silent. That was ... actually decent of him. But I still couldn't tell him what she'd told me. He'd start to think I was a demon who faked emotions. Like his last wife.

I could feel it already—the secret carving me up. The knowledge that would keep me alone.

Somewhere, deep down, I might be evil.

For once, I wanted to be alone in that little room. Maybe I didn't feel quite as scared of the ghost now.

If I'd crawled from the soil of an old ruin, maybe that bitch should be scared of me.

21

LILA

After walking back to the castle in the cold, I'd slept a few hours, curled up under the warm blankets.

By the time I woke up again, dinner was already waiting in the dumbwaiter, and I gobbled down the roast chicken and parsnips. Mum said I was always hungry, and she wasn't wrong about that. Maybe demons ate a lot. In any case, apparently, learning I *might* be evil hadn't killed my appetite.

As I ate, I considered the fact that I was now keeping a *real* secret from Samael. I was, perhaps, a demon. And if I told him that, he'd be certain my emotions were all completely fake.

Mum had said secrets made you feel alone, buried under the weight. But I would be keeping this one to myself regardless. This was not a secret like *I shagged the trumpet player from the Bibliotek band* or *I stole a stick of Mr. Wentworth's butter and ate the entire thing in one go and then threw up* or *every time I use the outhouse, I'm afraid a toilet-serpent will jump out and bite my arse*.

This wasn't even a *dreamt you tied me up and sexually tortured me* secret.

This was the kind of secret that would put my life in

danger. If this one got out—well, maybe the ghost's warning would come true. Maybe I'd find myself with my heart ripped out and my body tossed out the window.

But this was a real dilemma now. Because I was supposed to lead Samael to Finn and Alice, and Alice knew the truth about me. If we brought her back here, she might just tell him everything.

And then where would I be?

Dead in a moat.

I washed down my meal with a long sip of wine.

This was a very fine line I'd have to walk—working against the Free Men, trying to defeat them—while keeping secrets from my allies ... but maybe trying to silence our captive if it meant I'd end up dead.

I couldn't trust a single soul, which *was* painfully lonely.

Now, with the sun dipping lower over the west side of the river, my time was up. I had to get ready for the Wolfshunt festival. I'd have to figure something out—fast.

I had a beautiful dress to wear tonight. It was green, with long sleeves and a form-fitting bodice. I slipped into it, and the silk felt luxurious against my skin. It had a complicated set of buttons down the back, and I strained to reach behind myself to button them up. Once I had my gown on, I packed up my little bag, and the knife I'd stolen from the kitchen. I wasn't going anywhere without a weapon.

Just as I was grabbing my cloak, a knock sounded at the door.

When I opened it, I found Oswald standing in the hall, a silver tray in his hand. The torchlight wavered over his pale skin, green eyes, and dark hair. "For you, before you go off for a night out with the count."

I grinned. He'd brought me another fruit tart and a steaming coffee—along with three acorn necklaces.

I took the tray from his hand. "You are an angel. Not literally. Oh, it has cream and whiskey! I wanted to try that."

"How's your ghost?"

I arched an eyebrow. "Do you believe me now?"

He blew a curl out of his eyes. "I believe that you believe, so it's real enough."

I slid the tray onto the dresser, then poured a little cream and whiskey into the coffee. "Well, last night, the ghost beat me within an inch of my life and drowned me in moat water. But the acorns bloody work, as long as I have them on me. So thank you for bringing them." I pulled one of the acorn necklaces off the tray and tied it around my neck. "This little oak tree nut is the only thing keeping that ghost from murdering me."

I found Samael outside wearing a suit of deep charcoal gray, finely cut. It was too cold to go out without a cloak, but he wasn't wearing one anyway, just a bag over his shoulder. Without his hood on, I could see the entirety of his shockingly beautiful face, his high cheekbones sculpted by the setting sun. Ruddy light glinted in his pale eyes, and his auburn hair gleamed.

I pulled my cloak tighter around me. "Are we walking?"

"We'll fly over the river. We can land by the riverbank, then walk through the tunnel. I've brought masks."

"What are they?"

"Mine is a lion. Yours is a badger."

I frowned. "There wasn't anything more majestic than a badger?"

"The animal species isn't really important here, is it?" said Samael. "We're on a mission to stop an evil army. Consider the big picture."

"And yet I notice you're not choosing the badger, are you?"

"I was created eons ago from primordial clouds of stardust as a divine scourge of evil. I will not be the badger."

"Fine."

"There's a third option, if you like. There's a hedgehog." He leaned down and scooped me into his arms. I held on to him, enjoying the feel of his powerful body so close to me. His fingers were wrapped around my ribs and thighs.

His magnificent wings spread out behind him, the gold catching in the moonlight. Breathtaking. As his wings began to pound in the air, we lifted into the dark skies.

"Why three masks?" I asked.

"Sourial is joining us."

"Oh, good. I was starting to miss him."

"You *missed* him?" The corner of his mouth twitched. "He isn't fond of you, since you nearly murdered him."

"So that's why he hasn't been to see me."

"What do you miss about him?" Irritation laced his voice.

"It has been lonely in the room you locked me in."

He narrowed his eyes. "And you think of him when you're lonely?"

"I have thought of him once or twice. Mostly I think about the ghost of your dead wife trying to murder me. Not that you believe me, so I don't know why I try."

He went quiet, brooding. The jet-black eyelashes against his pale eyes really were mesmerizing. "My dead wife didn't have a soul," he said quietly. "No soul, no spirit, no ghost."

My throat tightened. "How can you be sure she didn't have a soul?"

"It's always been known among angels. When you see a demon, there's nothing beyond the surface, just emptiness behind the eyes. A demon can't feel real love, or even loathing. They pretend, sometimes, to feel emotions—

pretend to love, or to cry, or to be afraid. But demons live in a numb state." His voice sounded distant, dragged from darkness. "They're empty inside."

Either he was wrong or I wasn't a demon. Lord knew I had emotions.

His pale eyes pierced me. "Why are you so intensely interested in demons?"

"If we're going to fight demons, maybe we should understand them."

He frowned. "You don't need to understand them. Just to kill them. I've seen enough to know that if you let down your guard even for a second, if you make the mistake of trusting one for just a moment, they will destroy you. They leave trails of blood and destruction in their wake, always. If they have a soul, it's twisted beyond our imagination. I know they don't feel like we do. They don't have emotions. They don't have empathy. A demon could watch her child die in front of her and feel nothing. Underneath their numbness, they *yearn* to feel. It's what makes them do depraved things."

Sickness rose in my gut. "Being unable to feel doesn't mean you lack a soul."

Slowly, his gaze slid to me. "There is a reason you're asking about this, and it's not mere curiosity."

I pulled my gaze away from him. "Never mind." *Change the subject, Lila.* "Will I get to invite people to our fake wedding?"

"Your sister Alice? Your friend Finn? Any other Free Men you'd like to invite?"

"You really are tightly wound. Wonder why that is. A little pent-up frustration, perhaps?"

I heard a low growl rumble from his throat.

I peered down at the city as we flew, taking in the breathtaking view of the buildings—some dark stone, others bone white with delicate vaults and spires. We swept over Byzantine streets and old ruins overgrown with vines and flowers. It was hard not to marvel at this place and its mystery and wonders. The city was grim and heartbreakingly beautiful at the same time.

Maybe I loved it because I was born of its soil. I wanted to make Samael see it the way I did.

"Did you know that, thousands of years ago, a queen burned this city to the ground?" I asked. "Some said she was a sorceress. Because back then, men wouldn't allow women to rule, so they did unspeakable things to the queen and her daughters. In revenge, she slaughtered them all and lit the place on fire. And now, once a year, we crown a queen in the center of the city, on May first. Someone makes a crown of violet flowers called love-in-idleness. And she gets a sword, to symbolically slaughter anyone who wants to take her crown."

"How charming. Your heart is racing, by the way." His deep, velvety voice made me want to nestle in closer. "It happens whenever I fly with you. Are you afraid of heights?"

No. My heart raced when I was near him for a very different reason. "Not really. But didn't you tell me to be afraid of your reaper side?"

"I wouldn't kill you. I might slaughter everyone else. But you might be an exception."

Now, my heart was racing even faster. "Why?"

His eyes met mine, the look searing me. "Maybe I like your strange, rambling stories about Dovren ... the way you make this disgusting city come alive."

"Why did you take an arrow for me?"

"You're a mortal. You break easily. I made a calculation."

Except mortal babies didn't crawl from the soil, and mortal women didn't summon lethal tree branches from the earth.

But mortal, yes. We'd go with that for now.

Until we had Finn or Alice held captive, and then I'd have

to figure out what the fuck to do next so my cover wasn't blown.

We started to swoop down toward the city. "Lila," he murmured, "I can hear your heart racing again."

This time, there really was fear mixed in.

22

LILA

We soared down to the river, and I caught a glimpse of Sourial. On a stairwell landing, halfway up the embankment wall, he stood in the shadows. He was leaning against the door, brooding. With his arms crossed, face in shadows, I couldn't say he seemed thrilled to see me.

As we touched down on the top of the stairs, he glowered at me, eyes glinting in the dark. "Sweet Lila. I did think you were adorable until you caused my flesh to detach from my bones."

I swallowed hard. "Sorry about that. I'm glad you recovered." I glanced around the darkened river. I nodded at the door—our route into the underground passage. "Let's find the people who helped me make that poor decision, shall we?"

"Our disguises first," said Samael, withdrawing the masks again.

I pulled on my badger mask.

While the others donned their disguises, I yanked open the door to the underground tunnel. I crossed inside, and heard the angels follow. When the door closed behind us, I struggled to see in the dark. Only a distant torch lit the tunnel. It smelled like river mud in here, and the air felt heavy and wet. Nervousness fluttered through my gut—my two worlds about to collide again. My old mortal life, and the new one among angels. And when my two worlds crashed together, bad things tended to happen. I swallowed hard.

As we walked, our footfalls echoed off the ancient stone walls.

"I suppose it wasn't the worst thing," said Sourial from behind me. "Being immortal, I *do* get bored. One century is much like another. Fucking, fighting, invading new lands. I'd never been in a bomb blast before."

"Happy to help," I whispered.

I took a deep breath, my nerves jangling, and looked behind me in the tunnel. Nothing but darkness; no other people so far. Distantly, I heard the pounding of a drum, and muted voices carrying through the stone. As we moved closer to the sounds of the party, a disturbing thought was clawing at the back of my skull, trying to climb its way out. What would happen once we captured Alice? Would I let the angels torture her for information? She'd betrayed me, but she was my sister.

I was dreading what was about to happen. Especially Alice—I wasn't sure I could face her. Look her in the eye.

I closed my eyes, trying to force the disturbing thought from my mind. But there was the other worry—the one about my secret. If Alice knew, Finn might know as well.

I bit my lip, trying to work out exactly how I would explain it if Finn or Alice told them I was a demon. I cleared my throat.

"I want you both to know," I started in a low whisper, "that Finn and Alice might seem harmless. You might think him weak, easy to break. But I swear to you, he's a master of manipulation. He tried to turn me against you. They will try to turn you against me. You mustn't let them."

Was I laying the groundwork for my defense? Yes. But it just so happened that everything I was saying was also true. He *was* a master of manipulation. And if one of them started to talk ... if they was going to tell the angels ...

I couldn't let it happen. Once we got whatever information Samael needed to fight the Free Men, I had to shut them up before he blabbed.

"I think we'll be fine," said Sourial, sounding half-bored.

Apprehension crackled through my nerve endings as I envisioned how everything would go.

"We need a signal," I whispered, "so we can drag them out without anyone noticing."

"Why do we have to tread so carefully?" asked Sourial. "We could have brought our army and just killed anyone who objected."

"There will be kids there," I said sharply. "Most of the people there won't know that the Free Men are killers. Please don't turn this into a bloodbath."

"Bloodbath? I would *never.*" Sourial sounded genuinely offended.

"I remember what happened on Ernald's boat," I said.

"They deserved it," both angels replied in unison.

"We only need one person, right?" I asked.

"For now," said Samael. "Dragging out more than one person would likely attract too much notice. A signal is a good idea for discretion, too," he said quietly. "If they have an army of demons lurking in the shadows, discretion will be important. What would make a suitable signal?"

"Everyone gets drunk at these things," I said. "People sometimes spontaneously break into folk songs. I'll pretend to be sloshed and sing a folk song, but I'll change one word.

The song goes, 'Chop-a-head, under hill, the king is dead, the ravens kill.'"

"Why is everything in your country so disturbing?" asked Sourial. "Why can't you have normal festivals?"

I smiled. "There's something wicked in the soil." *Me.* "Okay, I'll change the last word, so you know it's me. Listen for 'the king is dead, the ravens *sing.*'"

"That doesn't even rhyme," Sourial scoffed.

"Good. Then it should stand out. That will be the signal that I'm near Finn. You both slip on over. Use your magical angel skills to subtly sneak him out, and we leave."

As we drew closer, I heard the music booming through the stones—the deep bass drum, the folk songs. I felt a twinge of nostalgia; my heart thumped at the familiarity of it all.

At the end of the tunnel, a round wooden door was inset in the stone wall. I pushed the door open, breathing in the once-familiar scent of the underground temple, soil and stone. And along with that, the smell of dozens of mortals—beer, sweat, and a bit of perfume.

Among the old columns and ruined stones, people were dancing to the music, their clothing bright as jewels. Colored lanterns were hung from the ceiling, casting gold and blue and red lights over the crowd. The revelers wore masks of wolves, butterflies, stags, and elk. Children ran around, squealing with delight. Some of them were in homemade masks of paper bags; others had beautiful masks with bright colors and gold paint.

The walls of the temple were engraved with images of skulls, and offerings and messages to the pagan god of death. Who, when I thought of it, was probably Samael. A shiver ran up my spine at the thought of centuries of Dovreners worshipping him.

In the center of the old temple, a wolf's head was impaled on a pike, with red ribbons running down from its neck.

Okay. The angels had a point. Everything in Dovren was slightly disturbing.

But I wasn't here for the festival anyway.

Already, I was feigning drunkenness, trying to look nonthreatening. Stumbling around, I sang to the folk songs. As I staggered around the ancient ruin, I scanned the crowd, looking out for any signs of Finn. He was taller than most, with a lumbering gate and golden hair.

I walked further into the crowd, moving between columns. When I saw a flash of flaxen hair in the distance, so pale it was almost white, every muscle in my body constricted. Alice's hair hung like a white flame down a dress of deep green.

Traitor.

Even with the raven mask on, I'd recognize her anywhere.

Anger flickered through my body. *You liar, Alice.*

She'd driven Mum insane, nearly got me killed, joined an army of killers. My fingers tightened into fists.

I started moving toward her, ready to break into my song. But as I approached, the music changed, and the crowd around me started whirling more frantically, jostling me.

As the music swelled higher, the crowd started to chant.

Albia awake! The storm is coming!

Bloody hell, they were all singing the Free Men songs now. A sick feeling curdled my stomach. How many of them were caught up in this cult? How many of them knew the truth about what the Free Men were doing? When I saw the children chanting, my nausea only intensified.

Frantically, I scanned the crowd for Alice. But as I looked for the pale blond hair, I saw something else that made my heart race. A crow I knew very well.

Ludd. Finn's crow swooped over my head, and I started to follow, stumbling through the revelers.

Finn was standing at the far side of the temple, taller than the rest of the crowd, when Ludd landed on his shoulder. He leaned against a carving of a winged angel, and his body looked tense, shoulders hunched, blond hair curling out behind his wolf mask.

I was so close to him now, only a few feet away.

Then, he pushed off from the wall. I stared as he raised his fist in the air, chanting along with the crowd.

"Albia first! Albia awake!" The deep sound of his voice carried over the crowd, louder and more fervent than the rest. A true believer.

My jaw clenched, fury snapping through my veins. *You betrayed me, Finn.*

I continued my pretense of stumbling, but behind my mask, I was searching the room for the best path out of here. We were nowhere near the entrance, which was a problem. If I called the angels here, how would they discreetly get Finn out without the entire crowd noticing?

A plan started to take root in the back of my mind.

I slipped back through the crowd and tried calling for Ludd, using the trick that Finn himself had taught me. My heart fluttered when I saw the bird swoop overhead. I kept up the ruse of drunkenness, pretending to stumble, still calling to Ludd.

The crow circled over my head while I led him toward the entrance.

As I got closer to the door, I turned to glance over my shoulder. My stomach clenched at the sight of Finn making his way through the crowd, looking up at his bird. For a moment, I felt a little twist of guilt in my heart. Right now, he looked like the old Finn. Easy to lead, attached to his crow. Bumbling and innocent.

But that wasn't him anymore. He'd grown into something twisted, something I could no longer love.

I glanced overhead, relieved to find Ludd right above me. Once I got closer to the entrance, I gave the signal: "*Chop-a-head, under hill, the king is dead, the ravens sing!*"

I sang it again, stealing a quick look behind me to make sure Finn was still following. I slowed my gait so he was just behind me.

From the shadows behind a column, Samael prowled forward in his lion mask, moving swiftly behind us both.

I gestured at Finn's chest with a wild swing of my wrist. Only then did Finn seem to notice me, stopping in his tracks.

Samael's move against him was swift and silent—a subtle but powerful blow to the back of his head. Finn slumped backward, falling into Samael.

Sourial swept in from the other side, slinging an arm around Finn's back, making it look like they were supporting a drunken friend. Ludd squawked, flapping his wings, but no one seemed to notice us.

As the two angels dragged Finn out the door, I found myself crushing the last little bit of guilt in my heart.

23

SAMAEL

In the dungeon of the Iron Fortress, I stared at the mortal man tied to a chair. He was still unconscious, his chest rising and falling slowly.

My instinct was to end him now—a swift and brutal death. But that wasn't why he was here. He was here to give me as much information as possible about the arrival of the Harrower.

A few candles hung in sconces in the walls, and the light wavered over his slumped body. Down here, there were no windows to let moonlight in—only a stone ceiling, curving above us, and cramped cells where mortals had once trapped each other. Kings and queens had been murdered in here, as well as countless traitors.

Today, I'd shed more blood. But at least it served a higher purpose.

The mortal's crow fluttered around the dungeon, squawking. I felt a pang of pity for the creature. He should not witness what was about to happen to his human friend, but I hadn't been able to get rid of him. He kept finding a way in.

I glanced behind me at Lila and found her expression

grim. She seemed very much on edge, ready to pounce at any moment.

"You shouldn't be here for this, Lila," I said.

"If you were betrayed by one of your closest friends, if you were left in the hands of the people he'd convinced you to attack, would you really miss the opportunity to see his interrogation?"

I turned back to the mortal, growing impatient now. I could snuff his life out as quickly as blowing out a candle, and with as little remorse. He had, after all, faked a photograph to convince Lila I'd murdered her sister.

Slowly, his eyes started to open. An expression of dawning dread crept over his features.

"Hello, mortal." I wanted him, first and foremost, to understand that he had no control here. "If you give me the answers to the questions I want, I may grant you a quick death instead of an excruciating one."

His cheeks paled. "Bloody hell. I ... I know very little. I'm probably not the person you want. I'm not important. You can't hurt me just because I don't know things!"

"No ... you aren't important." A plain statement of fact. "But you can tell me who is."

His gaze flicked behind me. "Lila. Lila. Lila!" He sounded hysterical, his voice ragged. "Lila is important. Why don't you start with her? *She* should be chained up. She's the one you should be hurting."

"This is nonsense," Lila hissed. "You liar."

"Lila is right." I got the impression he was saying whatever he needed to to save his own skin. I let my wings spread out wide behind me, blocking him from looking at Lila. "Who is actually important?"

Raw fear flickered over his features. I'd start with the easy questions. Once he got used to answering those, I'd move on to the *real* questions.

"When did you join the Free Men?" I asked.

Frantically, the mortal flexed his wrists, straining against the rope. "Not long ago. What do you want to know? I will tell you what I know, but it isn't much. Will you let me go if I tell you what you want to know? Will you let me live? I promise not to— to go back to the Free Men. I'll go to Clovia. Or the northern islands. I'll go—"

"Shut up."

His mouth closed fast. I breathed in, sensing something in him I hadn't noticed before.

Finn the mortal wasn't entirely mortal. I could smell it on him—the angelic side.

I went very still, feeling the darkness sliding through me, my predatory side emerging. "Tell me, nephilim. Why would you join an organization dedicated to the extinction of your kind?"

"*What?*" Lila shouted.

A little hope lit up his face. "So you know! I'm like one of you. You wouldn't hurt one of your own."

"That's not even close to true. Give me a real answer or I will rip out your tongue."

A vein pulsed in his forehead, and he started shaking. "Please don't do that! Fine ... fine!" he shouted. "You want to know why? I hate what I am. I hate being a monster. I thought I could make up for my poisoned blood by fighting with the Free Men. Your kind needs to stop taking our women. That's why I joined them. Please let me keep my tongue."

He was far too easy to break. He feared death intensely.

"My mother shagged an angel," he continued, stammering. "The angels take our women. My mother was a whore. I'm telling you the truth. You can let me free now. Please!"

"You never told me any of this," said Lila.

What a revolting person. "And will you send the Free Men to carve out your mother's lungs?"

He was shaking. "No. It would give me away."

"You make betrayal an art form. It's almost impressive."

"I was trying to avenge my father, after what my mother did to him. Not my birth father. The man who raised me. I'm telling you the truth. And Lila is every bit as much a whore—"

I hit him hard. The crack of fist against skull echoed off the stone arches.

Through a haze of primordial wrath, I struggled to think straight. I couldn't kill him before I got the chance to ask the important questions. I could feel my fury rising, the chains of fire moving around me.

When the mortal looked up at me again, terror shook his entire body. He began shrieking—high pitched, echoing. Maddening. His little mind couldn't handle my true form. Considering he was nephilim and Lila was mortal, it was amazing how much more easily he broke than her.

I gripped him by the throat, staring into his eyes. "Stay with me, Finn. Stay with me or your death will be both excruciating and undignified." I reached down and pressed my fingertips against his chest. "I want you to know that I can rip your heart out *very* slowly. So you will want to focus. When is the Night of the Harrowing?"

Trembling, he gaped at me. "I don't know. When they summon the Harrower. That's what they call it. The demon. I don't know. Please don't hurt me. Maybe it's soon? Yes, I think it's soon."

"When?"

Still stunned, his mouth worked soundlessly for a few moments. A bit of drool dripped down his chin. "Practicing the spell ... Baron is trying to master it. Yes, I've heard that. Please. I don't want to die."

"Where is the Baron?"

"He's ... I don't know, exactly ..." he stammered. "I don't know who he is. I don't even know if it's a man. It's their biggest secret. Only the highest level knows. I'm not ready to die yet. Lila should be here instead of me. You're targeting the wrong person. She's evil."

"See?" Lila blurted. "He's trying to turn you against me."

With a single swift movement, I jabbed my fingertips against his ribs, breaking one of them in a way that would puncture his lung.

His eyes went wide, and he gasped. Pain would be tearing his mind apart now. I glanced behind me, catching a glimpse of Lila standing by Sourial's side. Her expression looked grim, body tense, eyes locked on her former friend.

I didn't like Lila to see this side of me—the brutality that came so naturally to me. I was the being who snapped ribs and necks, who expertly used pain as a tool. But maybe it was best if she understood who I really was.

In the world that we lived in—the one created by mortals—someone had to wield the blade to keep order. Someone had to crack the bones, to sever the heads to protect the vulnerable. I would be that person. The monster cloaked in horror, reviled, soaked in blood.

And I would gladly deliver death to the wicked, because that was what I was made for.

"Who is the highest level?" I asked.

"They use code names. Secrets. So many secrets. Everyone has a code name. I know Alice, of course. Lila's sister. Except not sisters by blood. They're not alike. Not at all ..." He struggled and gasped, nearly moaning with the pain. "Alice is important. You should find her! Bring her here. Instead of me. I can help you find her."

"Is she at the highest level?" Sourial's voice boomed from behind me.

The nephilim was still stunned with terror as he looked up at me. "Yes. She is, yes."

If he was telling the truth, which he might not be, Alice would know who the Baron was. But would she break as easily?

"Where do I find her?"

"I don't know where she's staying. I only know she sometimes meets them in ..." He bit his lip, visibly trying to shut himself up.

Another swift jab to his chest broke another rib. His breathing was now labored, panicked.

"They call it the telescope of fire," he grunted. "Telescope of fire!"

Was he just uttering nonsense? "The telescope of fire."

"It's what they call it. It's where they meet."

"What does Alice look like?" I asked.

I'd already gotten her description from Lila, but I wanted to know if their stories matched up. "Taller than Lila. Pale. Flaxen hair. Gray eyes. Black eyebrows. She wears a dark green coat."

Exactly as Lila had described. Good.

"Does the Baron meet with her at the telescope of fire?" Sourial barked.

Finn shook his head. "I don't know. I'd tell you if I knew who he was, but they haven't told me. I only know he's in Dovren."

"Where in Dovren?" Sourial shouted from the shadows.

Finn looked lost, delirious as he stared up at me—so gripped with horror and agony that he could no longer form a coherent thought. "Ding, dong, bell. Put him in the well. Why put him in? Not enough gin—"

"Shut up," I said in a low voice. He was jabbering now. I pressed a little harder against his ribs. "What exactly do they have planned for the Night of the Harrowing?"

He sucked in a panicked breath. "Raise Lilith. They've made a bargain with her already. They will summon her and use her to kill all the unworthy. The monsters. The whores. The mongrels. Anyone who helps them. I'd be on the right side, you see? They'd let me live."

Hearing her name spoken aloud sent a chill through my blood. "When?" I tried this question again.

His mouth opened and closed silently a few times, and then he blurted, "Close. And then it will all be over. There is a spy in your court."

I pushed harder, cracking another one of his ribs. "Who?"

"Lila."

"He's lying!" she shouted.

Every one of my muscles froze. I felt darkness slipping out of me, chilling the room with a glacial frost. The crow flew overhead, crying out.

"It's not true," she said from behind me. "I told you he would do this. I told you he would try to turn us against each other."

I ignored her, staring at the nephilim. "Lila," I repeated.

"I can tell you about Lila. I know. She's not what you think. She's not even mortal."

If he was going to call her a whore again, I might just snap his neck. But perhaps this was worth hearing. "Not mortal?"

"This is obviously nonsense," raged Lila from behind me. "Don't let him mess with your head!"

"Sourial," I barked. "Take her out of here."

"She's not mortal!" shouted Finn. "She should be locked up! She's lying to you!"

"He's going to manipulate you!" Lila sounded nearly as frantic as he did. "He splits people apart, don't you see?"

"Not mortal?" I asked, pressing my fingertips against one of his broken ribs.

"When you realize ..." he stammered. "You will want to kill her. She's your real enemy. Pure evil."

Why did I feel as if there were a little kernel of truth under this babbling?

Lila shouted again, "He's lying!"

"She's the one you want!" The boy was shrieking at this point. "Not me!"

Furious, I whirled to see Sourial trying to drag Lila from the room. She was struggling against him, kicking and elbowing him. I could see him restraining himself, trying not to hurt her. If he didn't care for her wellbeing, this would be over by now. She'd be lying in a heap on the floor.

But more importantly—what the fuck was she doing?

Darkness swept over me as I watched her break free and pull her knife from her bag.

We weren't truly on the same side, were we?

24

LILA

I gripped the knife hard, my body vibrating with ferocity. A pressure was rising in my skull, spiked and ragged. I felt as if thorny vines were blooming inside my mind, forcing out my own thoughts. Ludd was screeching, as if he sensed something terrible was about to happen. As if he knew that I needed to keep Finn quiet.

A dark side of me was rising. I thought the ghost might be stoking it—she wanted me to silence Finn.

There was only one way to stop this pressure. I had to keep the secrets sealed tight. The ghost demanded it.

Kill or be killed. Her voice boomed in my thoughts, a voice that wasn't quite my own. She terrified me, yes, but she was also warning me. If I wanted to live, Finn had to die. Now.

The angels could not know what I was. Finn had told them I was a spy. What if they discovered I was a demon?

If Samael knew the truth about me, I'd be the one strapped to the chair, ribs broken. He believed demons did not have souls, that their emotions were entirely feigned. And it seemed like I could be a demon. There was no guilt in hurting a soulless creature who couldn't feel, was there?

The world dimmed around me until I saw only my target.

Kill or be killed, the ghost sang.

I threw the knife so fast neither of the angels had the chance to stop me. It struck Finn in the jugular, and blood poured from his throat. Dead.

But they weren't thinking about that, no. They were staring at me with uncomprehending bafflement. Shadows seemed to whirl around Samael, then a chill swept through the room; frost spread through the air.

At least my mind was free of the pressure. I started to catch my breath, shocked at what I'd just done. I'd just killed Finn. My throat tightened, and I tried not to think about what he'd been like as a kid, or how we'd play hide and seek around the market stall. How we'd hunted for treasure together on the muddy river bank. It was nearly impossible to reconcile that little boy with this creature who'd called me a whore.

With my entire body shaking, I closed my eyes, trying to block out the angels' shouting. I felt hollow, broken. I felt as if I'd killed a part of myself—the innocent part of me.

Strange to think I'd never really known Finn the way I thought I had. He never told me about his mum and dad, that he was a nephilim. Clutching my stomach, I wanted to be sick.

How dreadfully sad that he hated himself that much, that he would join the Free Men.

I'd killed him to silence him. How much had that been the darkness within me, and how much had been the ghost trying to influence me? I opened my eyes again, confronted by the two furious faces of the angels.

"Let me guess." The ice in Samael's voice was a stark contrast to the fire in his eyes. "A ghost told you to do that. Or do you have some other lie in mind this time?"

"I told you he would try to turn you against me," I said.

"You were letting him manipulate you. He's cleverer than you'd think. You learned everything you needed to know. Alice is important, and the telescope of fire. It was all he knew. Anything after that was just going to be his attempt to get revenge on me."

"You have very little faith in us," said Sourial. "It's astounding. Perhaps you are a spy."

"See? He's in your head."

"How did you learn magic?" asked Samael in a deep, quiet tone that thrummed over my skin.

Ludd fluttered around the room, panicked.

"I didn't," I said in a small voice.

"Alice was there at the festival, wasn't she?" said Sourial, eyes narrowing. "She's higher up, but you led us to Finn. The captive of lesser value. Seems convenient."

Frustration crackled through me. "She disappeared into the crowd. That was it. Finn was easier to lure. I didn't know she was important until now."

Samael's gaze bored into me. "This time, Sourial, when we lock the door, we must make sure she cannot get out."

※

I PACED IN MY LOCKED ROOM, FEELING LIKE A CAGED BIRD. The door had been bolted over with metal—a lock I couldn't pick. The windows, too; bolted shut.

I thought I'd been in here six days—just me and Ludd, who'd followed after me, screeching at me in his corvid language. I was sure it was a litany of curses. The poor thing still screeched whenever I got near, terrified of me.

I turned, staring at the crow. He sat perched on the windowsill, dark eyes watching my every movement. "Stop looking at me like that. You feathery little judge. Sanctimonious corvid fiend."

He cocked his head, and I swear his eyes narrowed with hatred.

I took a tentative step closer. "How do I win back your affection? You are my only friend here. You and Jenny. My two bird friends."

Hatred gleamed in his dark eyes.

I took another step closer to him, the floorboards creaking beneath my feet. His black eyes stayed fixed on me. Quietly, I cooed, trying to soothe him. "Ludd. I give you food, remember? It's just you and me, my friend."

One more step—

He squawked, flapping his wings. Furious.

I sighed. "Look, I've tried to tell you. Your best friend wasn't the person you thought he was, Ludd. He didn't deserve you. He was a *very* bad person, and he was trying to get me killed. So I did what I had to do to survive. Sometimes it's kill or be killed, you know? You'd understand if you could understand the words I was saying."

Ludd puffed out his chest, fluttering his wings again.

I pivoted, stalking back the other way. In addition to Ludd, I had the books to keep me company, and I'd gotten much better at reading. One by one, I'd been working my way through the small library at my disposal. Slowly, painstakingly —but I was reading, nonetheless. Knowledge was power.

With each page, I understood more.

In fact, I almost felt as if that dark presence in my mind was helping me learn. I'd done what she wanted, and she'd stopped attacking me.

I scanned one of the bookshelves, looking for something new. Some of the books were histories of Albian wars. Some were romances. But the best—and most dreadful—find of all was a catalogue of the history of demons. It was an enormous book, detailing every horrific thing the demons had ever done to mortals over the years.

I learned that demons amused themselves by leaving mortals lovesick, feeding off heartbreak. Some started wars between nations so they could thrive off the pain, the anger and conflict.

The book also claimed that demons did not have emotions—and that was certainly perplexing, because I had a *lot* of pent-up emotions. I must have at least one mortal parent. Maybe half-demons weren't so bad?

As I knelt over the book, I heard the creaking of the dumbwaiter. My stomach rumbled. The three meals were the high points of my day.

I crossed to the dumbwaiter and lifted the wooden door. My mouth watered at the sight of poached salmon with roasted carrots and potatoes. Someone had left more acorns on the tray, a small bottle of chilled white wine, and another fruit tart.

I dropped the demon book onto the table, sliding my plate next to it. I poured myself a glass of wine and flipped through the book as I ate, spearing salmon and potatoes with my fork while I read about the different types of demons—the incubi, the succubi, the demons of possession, the demons who'd come from fallen angels that had turned evil.

As I read, I could hardly focus on what I was eating, my mind occupied with page after page of the demons' wickedness. And when I got to a page with a picture of a wild-haired demon, I dropped my fork. She was facing away from the viewer, her hair like writhing snakes.

She wore a dress of pale green and gold, her body surrounded by illustrations of ruby red fruit and flowers on the vines. She held one of the fruits in her hand—red with seeds, just like the fruit I was given every night.

But it was the word at the top of the page that struck dread into my heart. *The Harrower*.

The text beneath her image read: *The Harrower has the*

power to call life from the earth. She can make the dead live again. She can raise plants from the soil and control them at will.

My blood went cold.

That sounded a *lot* like the power I had.

At the bottom of the page, I found a symbol that made my heart pound harder. It was the same symbol I'd seen several times now—the crescent moon wrapped in vines. The one that had appeared on my wrist.

There was no mistaking this. I was connected to the Harrower, and she had lived here once. Maybe she was my real mother, or maybe I was simply a dead creature she'd summoned from the earth using her powers. A buried baby she'd brought to life again—one who could summon plants as she had.

Somehow, we were connected. Mum had told Alice about how I was found—black eyes, crawling from the dirt. Alice and Finn worked together. Alice must have told him about me, so he'd probably felt no guilt at all when he set me up to be killed in Castle Hades. What did he care for a demon life?

As the sun set, it cast flaming coral rays over the page. I stared at it, entranced and horrified at the same time. Then, I traced my fingertips over the Harrower.

She made things come to life again. That didn't seem like an evil power, did it?

But Finn said she had made a deal with the Free Men already. That was evil.

A voice started to flutter like moth wings around my head. *Look at yourself, Lila. Your secret won't stay buried for long, and Samael is the one who brings down the sword. He's the person who finishes the job.*

Ludd was squawking even louder than usual now, completely terrified of me. Slowly, with a hammering heart, I stood and crossed to the mirror.

There, the world tilted beneath me.

My face had transformed—eyes black as jet, my hair writhing around my head. My skin was pale, ashen.

In the reflection, my mouth moved. *"This is the real you, Lila,"* the vision spoke. *"And you can fight it and lose, or you can accept what you were born to do. Kill Samael."*

With an iron will, I mastered control of my own thoughts. "Who is the Harrower?"

I stared as the reflection moved, coming to life from the mirror. My own arm reached from the looking glass and ripped the acorn charm from my throat.

Before I could react, the reflection gripped me by the neck, squeezing hard. *"I hurt you because you're soft. You'd never survive without me."*

I felt my lungs filling with murky water again. Panic snapped through my mind.

"You need to feel what it's like to die," she hissed. "You need to be ready to fight back."

I brought my knee up hard into her gut, knocking her back and moving swiftly away. But as I did, the ghost grabbed me from behind, by the hair, by the neck. Her claw-like fingers were digging into my throat.

"You're not as afraid of Samael as you should be." She squeezed tighter, her damp, cold fingers pressing my windpipe shut. "I didn't see it coming when he killed me. You think he looks at you sometimes with affection. You think he respects you. Admires you, even. Little signs that he cares. But inside, he feels nothing. Death drives him, seduces him. It is what he was made for. You've seen his true face. You've seen what he is. Do not be lured in by his beauty, because you will end up drowning in the moat."

The phantom was crushing my throat, robbing me of breath. I couldn't speak anymore. Instead of trying to talk, I slammed my elbow hard into her ribs. Once, twice—

She only pressed harder on my throat. Delirious, I felt

sludgy water covering my body from my feet upward. I was freezing, shivering.

She whispered in my ear. "When he decides you are not worthy of him, that he cannot accept what you are, he will snap your little ribs. He will rip your heart out of your chest, then toss your body in the moat. He will treat you like you are nothing more than rubbish. He doesn't want you as his wife; he needs you to fulfill a role. And once the part is played, you will sink into the muck. Your pretty face will rot. Your body will fester and grow cold. Forgotten. No one will remember you. Kill or be killed."

Fury raged in me like a storm. She said she was warning me, but she just wanted to hurt me.

I'm not the weakling you think I am, bitch.

I reached behind my head, grabbing her hard by the neck. I shoved my hips back into her and bent sharply forward, flipping her over me.

Despite gasping for breath, I slammed her down on the table. Her body splintered the wood, and the acorns rolled across the floor. I snatched them from the ground, and stuffed them into her mouth.

She went still, her body convulsing.

Behind her dark hair, I got glimpses of her face—ashen skin, dark veins over her cheeks, black eyes.

The acorns were weakening her, making her shake. I clamped her mouth shut, forcing them in. "Listen, my ghostly friend. I've got an endless supply of acorns. They keep giving them to me here. It's quite nice, isn't it? They're looking after me, even if I'm locked up."

Her dark eyes went wide, hands grasping.

"If there is something you want me to understand, why don't you make yourself useful? Why not tell me what you want me to know *in words?*" I roared the last bit. "When I let you open your mouth again, either tell me what the fuck is going on," I added, "or use your ghost powers to open the door and let me out. And if you open the locked room for me, maybe I can figure things out for myself. Because that's the key to it all, isn't it? The symbols. The Raven King. The Harrower. That's where it all starts, right? That room. Let me in on the secrets. Because I know what a secret can do to someone. They can bury you alive."

I released my grip on her and watched as she scrambled up from the floor, choking and spitting out the acorns. Stumbling, she crossed to the door.

She slammed her fist into the wood, over and over, until she splintered it. As she punched, fiery pain spread over my own knuckles. I grimaced, cradling my fist.

At last, she had punched a hole in the door. Glaring at me, she slipped her arm through the hole, unlatched the lock, and slid the bar over.

Then, she flickered out of existence.

I looked down at my hand. My knuckles were bleeding. I touched my throat, feeling the bruises already starting to rise.

But the door was open, and the ghost was leading me to that room—the one where she used to live. I slipped out into the dark hallway.

This was dangerous, I knew. But I had to find out the truth, and I was sure I'd find it there.

25

SAMAEL

I cracked open the book on my desk—a history of Dovren in the seventeenth century. Candlelight warmed the room, and steam curled from a cup of hot tea on my desk.

I didn't want the tea. I wanted the deep, smoky whiskey next to it. Already, I'd spent days searching for references to a telescope. Landmarks of Dovren, universities, laboratories. I'd found many telescopes, but none of them seemed like suitable meeting spots for people who wanted to stay hidden. And none of them had anything to do with fire.

I poured myself a glass of whiskey and took a sip, letting it roll over my tongue. Rich and peaty.

My lovely bride knew this city inside and out. Lila understood the magic of the place. She looked at the grim and crumbling ruins of a once-glorious world and saw something that still shone with beauty. She understood the hearts of the people who lived here in a way I never had. In the two decades since I'd lived in Dovren, I'd never thought much about those living in the slums to the northeast of me—not until I'd met Lila. Now, I'd ordered the Clovian soldiers to start delivering food to them, making meals available for families who were starving in the East End.

She loved this city the way a parent loved a child. She would be my best source of information.

Except that she wasn't telling me the truth. It was clear to me that she was keeping secrets, and that meant I couldn't trust her.

I turned another page to find an illustration of Dovren burning, flames curling into a night sky. It looked eerily like the Night of the Harrowing that the Free Men had planned—a fiery purge to cleanse the city.

As I stared at the image, I could almost hear the screams, and my muscles tightened. But this image depicted the past, not the future. Hundreds of years ago, half of Dovren had burned to ash in a night known as the Great Incineration. Flames had raged through the streets, just as they would again if I didn't stop the Free Men.

The mortals, in all their wisdom, had blamed the fire on divine retribution for the sin of gluttony. They'd even created a statue of a plump boy to commemorate it—a reminder not to eat too many pies, erected near the butchers' market. As an instrument of God, I could confirm divine retribution did not depend on the eating of pies.

Later, when one of the Albian kings had decided to invade Clovia, he'd rewritten the story. The new story was that Clovians had set the fire. It was a justification for the war, of course.

I turned the page—another image of the Great Incineration, from the perspective of the river. The next page depicted an enormous column that speared the night sky, a monument to the death and destruction of the fire. The stars were drawn strangely large and prominent in the image, forming a dome around the top.

I stared at it. Most monuments in the city featured

statues of monarchs at the top. Why would a king fund construction of a memorial if it wasn't going to glorify him? But this one—this had nothing. And it had been built just about the time that primitive telescopes were invented.

Long and thin, the shape of the column would be perfect for observing the stars. With lenses, it could function as an enormous telescope.

I didn't know if this was it, but it was worth investigating.

IN THE WINDING MAZE OF DOVREN'S STREETS, I STOOD before the monument to the Incineration. It stood at the base of a hill, in the center of five cobblestone streets that jutted from it like spokes in a wheel.

In the stone at the bottom of the monument, someone had chipped away at the cautions about gluttony and carved instead a description of evil Clovians.

With a glance over my shoulder, I crossed to the enormous metal door at the base and pulled it open to reveal a circular room. Only a stream of moonlight from the top lit it. When I looked up, I found dizzying swirls of spiral staircases sweeping up to the oculus. This could be used for observations.

Was this their meeting spot?

When I looked beneath my feet, I found a nearly imperceptible circular carving in the wooden floor. Something hidden?

I shifted toward the edge and surveyed the space, looking for something like a lever or a button. At last, near the door, I found an indentation carved in the stone, with a star marking it. When I pressed on it, the sound of turning gears filled the base of the stairwell, and a wooden hatch rose from the floor. I slid the covering out of the way and peered down.

RAPTURE

More spiral stairs swooped down below me. Interesting.

I squeezed through the opening, just barely making it through, then descended into the darkness.

When I got to the bottom at last, I found myself in a sort of primitive laboratory of stone. It smelled musty and damp down here. Silver light streamed from the opening I'd climbed through.

A lever jutted from one of the walls, and curiosity compelled me to pull it. When I did, a whirring noise filled the room, the sound of chains and gears creaking behind the walls. I stared above me as a lens slid into place at the top of the laboratory.

As I stared up at the canopy of starry sky so crystal clear before me, my chest ached. I didn't remember it, but I could feel that that sky had once been my own. I remembered nothing of my life before the fall. I didn't even know if God was real or not. I didn't know who made the rules or why. Falling meant that understanding was torn from you, and you were left to grapple around in the dirt with the other beasts, a life of pain with no purpose.

And yet, hadn't mortals found a purpose here on the wretched earth. They'd constructed brilliant contraptions like this. Sometimes, mortals managed to stun me with the angelic nature of their intellect. It was easy to forget what they were capable of.

Maybe they longed for the stars like I did. Maybe they felt incomplete as I did, yearning for wholeness in the heavens. Perhaps they felt ripped in two, at war with themselves, just like I did.

I pushed the lever up on the side of the wall, and watched the lens slide away again.

This must be the place—a telescope of fire. I'd be sending a few spies to linger in the shadows around this place, watching for anyone coming in and out.

For the first time, I was making some actual headway in finding the Baron. I was on the right path at last.

As I climbed the stairs, I wondered what Lila was doing in her room. Whether or not she was lying, my dreams still told me I had to marry her. It was just that marrying Lila meant I'd have to actually speak to her again. I'd have to look her in the eyes and ask her to tell me the truth about everything. If she was going to be on my side through this, as my dreams suggested, we would need to trust each other.

As soon as I returned to the castle, I would speak to her again.

I hoisted myself out of the opening, then stood. With a push of the button, I closed the hatch.

If I were honest with myself, I'd also been keeping plenty of secrets from Lila. I'd certainly left out a few key details about my past. Maybe that was the place to start.

I pushed through the door and into the night, feeling the wind rush over me. It seemed there *was* magic in this city if you knew where to look, just like Lila had said. With one last glance back at the telescope of fire, I pulled my cowl over my head. I slipped into the shadows, stalking through the cobbled streets.

But there ahead of me—someone caught my eye.

A woman walked through the streets, and my gaze homed in on her. I caught the dark eyebrows, a stark contrast to her pale blond hair. She was walking on the other side of the cobbled street with her hands in her pockets. Black eyebrows, flaxen hair. Heading right for the monument.

Alice.

As I moved for her, her head flicked up, and she caught my gaze. Her pale eyes widened, and she turned to run, sprinting back up the narrow, cobbled hill. As she did, she screamed, "Angel!"

A fleeing enemy ignited my predatory instincts, and I felt

cold darkness sliding through me. She wasn't the sort of mortal who created beauty like I'd just seen. She was the kind who'd burn it all down.

A dark smile curled my lips as I watched her run, screaming for help. I enjoyed the chase a little too much.

My wings spread out behind me and pounded the air. But as I lifted into the skies, two more mortals rounded the corner at the top of the hill. One of them raised a bow, aiming at me before unleashing his arrow. I swerved to try to avoid it, but it ripped through one of my wings.

Pain shot through my bones, into my back. There was nothing more excruciating than an injured wing, and it was still recovering from the demon attack. I veered down to the ground, fury burning away the pain.

As I careened toward the earth, another arrow shot straight into my chest, near my shoulder. I landed ungracefully, slamming down hard enough that I fell to my knees. When I looked up, I could feel my true face rising.

Wrath slid through my veins; my thoughts dimmed. As if from a distance, I watched myself rise to my feet. I ripped the arrow from my chest with a snarl.

There were more mortals running closer to me, screaming, "Albia awake! Kill the monsters!"

And they were right—right now, I was a monster. Because I wasn't just the Angel of Death anymore. The reaper in me was starting to rise, and I wanted to rip them all apart one by one.

I was vaguely aware of another arrow slamming into my gut, but it didn't matter. I was beyond pain now; King of the Fallen, moving for them like a wind of death. Carving my sword through the air, I cut through one of the bows. Then I brought Asmodai down through the arms of the man who held it. He screamed in horror, and I whirled, scanning for the next enemy.

I tuned out their screaming. This was a macabre dance of death, and I was the only one who knew the steps. I lost myself in the violence, feeling it feed me, filling the emptiness. Blood ran down the cobblestones in little rivulets.

And when I was done, only one person remained.

Alice. My bride's sister.

"You're a monster," she stammered.

"As are you." I lifted her by the throat. "But only one of us will survive in the end."

Terror beamed in her pale eyes. I wanted to tear her head from her body, but in the recesses of my mind, I remembered I needed to keep her alive. I needed her for questioning.

As her jaw went slack, I realized she'd gone unconscious too fast. Had I driven her mad? I dropped my grip on her. I'd wanted her knocked out, but that had been nearly immediate. Some of the rage was sliding out of my body now, and I crouched down by her side. She looked dead.

The air smelled sharply of bitter almonds. I pulled open her mouth. There, resting on her tongue, was a small capsule. She'd poisoned herself to escape me.

My blood roared in my ears.

When I pressed my fingertips against her throat, I felt a faint pulse. There was still time, then.

As I turned to survey the street, I found carnage spread out around me. Bewildered, I stared at the torn bodies. I hardly remembered killing them at all. My worst reaper instincts had taken over, and I'd simply blacked out.

No wonder Alice had chosen the poison.

I stared at a rivulet of red streaming between the cobblestones. For the first time, I was starting to think my dreams were wrong.

Maybe someone like me should not be king at all.

26

LILA

As I walked through the candlelit stone halls, Samael's face kept flitting through my mind. Despite his lethal exterior, I knew his heart was good. Under his scary side, he wanted to keep the city safe from pure evil. It was just that his methods were sometimes brutal.

But the real question was, would he be able to see the same was true of me? Would he see that, underneath, my heart was good?

I wasn't so confident.

When I got to the ghost's room, I found the door unlocked, and I slipped inside. The setting sun stained the room with ruby and violet. In the lurid sunlight, something caught my eye: the boutonnieres, hung upside down from the wall on ribbons. Samael had dried them all so he could keep them. I was sure they were the same ones—daises, corn-cockle, foxglove, and those beautiful bluebells.

Strangely, he'd even improved them. Now, they were wrapped in silver ribbon, and he'd added something even more beautiful—little feathers from the downy part of his wings, black shot through with gold veins.

There was something touching about this. Thinking of Samael, Venom of God, keeping that little girl's wonky boutonnieres, trying to fix them. What on earth had made the Angel of Death interested in *crafting?*

But this wasn't why I'd come.

I wanted to find out about the Harrower. My gaze flicked up at her symbol entwined with the raven. Simple and elegant lines.

I climbed onto the dresser. If ever I needed the help of the Raven King, it was now.

I touched the carving, pressing my palm against the symbol of the raven. As I closed my eyes, I felt the city's magic in this stone.

Then, I knocked three times. "Raven King, give me answers."

With the words out of my mouth, I felt a familiar, intense power rippling over me. It was the same one I felt when I walked through Dovren's streets, the dormant magic under the stones. It felt powerful, protective, deeply connected to me. And now, it was stronger than ever. I was about to get my answers.

With a racing pulse, I climbed down from the dresser and slowly turned.

There, in the far corner of the room, sat a king on a throne.

His hair gleamed silver, draped over a black cloak with a feathered collar. His skin was pale and smooth, with green eyes that glittered like jewels. Beautiful ... and oddly familiar. A silver crown rested on his head and a raven perched on his shoulder.

I could hardly breathe.

I'd thought he might answer me. What I hadn't expected was to see him here before me.

"Raven King," I whispered.

"You found me, my love?" He spoke in Ancient Albian. And somehow, I understood it.

I stared at him, shock running through my body. The man I'd been praying to all these years was right in front of me, beautiful as hell.

I let out a breath. "The feel of your magic is very familiar."

He rose from his throne, towering over the room in his black cape and clothes. "Have you come to understand what you are?"

"I think I'm connected to the Harrower," I whispered. "Either that or I've gone completely mad."

"You've not gone mad." His deep, melodic voice thrummed along my skin, and his gaze was so intense it made my heart race.

"I thought maybe the Harrower created me."

"Lilith. Her name is Lilith."

The name made me shudder with a buried recognition. "Did she raise me from the soil?"

He took a step closer to me. "In a way."

"What do you mean?"

"You must understand that what is written about demons is not entirely true. Demons can feel more strongly than anyone. But when it gets too much for them, they suppress their emotions. They turn them off. They don't feel a thing."

"What am I? A demon? What are you?" My mind was flooded with all this information; I could hardly take in what was happening.

"I was mortal," he said. "The first king to unite Albia. Lilith was my queen. She was a demon, yes. But she loved me. She'd carve that wherever she lived, even long after I died." Sorrow gleamed in his eyes as he gestured at the carving—the raven and the moon. "When I grew sick with the black fever, she knew I was going to die. And I knew what she planned to do. She would raise me from the dead again. I wouldn't let her."

I drew a shaky breath. "Why not?"

"I wouldn't come back the same. And I wanted a city to grow from my death. I wanted my spirit to live in the soil, in the trees and stones. If she raised me again, I'd be just another demon. So, I asked her to bury my head. It lays in the hill under Castle Hades. My death has fed this city with my power."

I took a deep, shaking breath. "What happened to the Harrower—Lilith? Did she turn evil?"

"Long after I died, about a thousand years ago, she was captured by mortals and put in chains. I could hear her crying for me, but I could not do a thing. They called her the devil's whore. They tortured her for months. They burned her over and over again, telling her they must purify her. Through the torture and burnings, her mind snapped. Her emotions shut off. But she didn't die. The only way to kill a demon is to cut out her heart. She endured the most excruciating torture, and she grew to loathe mortals."

Pity twisted my heart. "That's terrible."

Shadows slid through his eyes, his expression haunted. "They turned her into something darker."

I stared. "And she ended up here. In this room."

"She was engaged to Samael for a time. She was using him." He looked at the carving, his expression mournful. "As you can see, she still thought of me. Underneath the icy surface of her emotions, she thought of me."

My fingers twitched. "She's been visiting me in my room. She certainly seems twisted. How am I connected to her?"

He took another step closer. Wind rushed through the broken window, toying with his silver hair. He reached for my face, brushing the back of his knuckles against my cheek. "I need you to know that I will always answer your call, Lilith. I didn't know how, all those centuries ago. But I know now." Dark pain tinged his quiet voice, and he sounded like he was speaking from the depths of hell. "Even if I don't always show up like this, I can hear you. I can give you magic."

I staggered back. "What did you say?" Ice slid through my veins. "Why did you call me Lilith?"

"You are Lilith. Grown from the earth, in the same city where my head lays buried. I saw to it that you came back, because the world needed you. You're mortal now, but that will change. When the Free Men work their magic, your demonic powers will be restored. And your memories, too."

Horror slid through my bones. "What? No. No! I don't want to change."

"You can't fight the Free Men without more power."

"But she's evil."

"Your soul is not evil. You must fight through her memories."

I froze, and a wave of horror washed over me. "So ... *I'm* the Harrower? The evil creature that will summon demons from the earth? The one Samael has been trying to kill? I don't understand. How will I be summoned?"

The Raven King put a finger to his lips, then nodded at the door.

When I turned to look at it, I found Samael looming in the doorframe.

And when I turned back to the Raven King, he'd gone.

27

SAMAEL

The setting sun beamed through the window, lighting her up from behind. I wondered what she'd do if she knew her sister was here in the dungeon, in chains.

In the dying light, her hair seemed to ignite with fiery colors. Her fragile, mortal beauty was deceptive. Under her delicate exterior, she was fire and iron.

And she was running rings round me—again.

"How did you get out?" I asked.

She looked pale, terrified. "Thing is, you wouldn't believe me if I told you."

"Try me."

She looked down at her fist. Her knuckles were bleeding. "The ghost opened my door."

I had told Lila that I'd never believe her about the ghost—the same lie she'd used in Castle Hades. And yet here she was, using that same lie. Only an idiot would do that. And Lila was no idiot.

As much as I'd resisted it, maybe I had to face the possibility that she could be telling the truth this time.

I took a step closer, feeling each one of my muscles tensing. Fierce bruises bloomed on her neck—maroon, violet. It looked like someone had tried to kill her. My protective instincts roared to the surface.

"Who did that to you?" I asked quietly. I felt like I was splitting in two.

"Lilith."

She'd been in danger, and I'd refused to believe her. "The ghost?"

She stared at me, fear gleaming in her eyes. Never before had she looked so terrified of me. That look was like ice shattering in my heart.

"What happened to your neck?" I pressed. "She tried to choke you?"

No answer again. Wind from the broken window whistled into the room, rustling the drying flowers on the wall.

I hated this room. The very place was cursed with Lilith's malign presence, and it hung like a miasma over every surface. I couldn't explain why I'd come in here to dry the boutonnieres. I supposed I'd wanted to try to add a little humanity to the place—like a charm against Lilith's evil. And Lila and that little girl seemed so perfectly human.

What a strange thing humanity was—all at once it was brutal and brilliant and idiotic and heartbreaking.

"I'm going to tell you the whole truth." She looked like she was about to snap, her shoulders hunched, jaw tight. Her eyes shone with a ferocious expression. "Because maybe I need to be stopped. If I need to be stopped ..." she sputtered. "You have to do it."

"What are you talking about?" I wondered if she was, in fact, losing her mind. "Stop what?"

She stared at me, and the wind rushed in again through the broken window, whipping her hair in front of her face.

Her dark eyes seemed to be pleading with me. "No more secrets. Because maybe I'm not the good guy."

All of a sudden I felt an overwhelming need to protect her. "Explain."

"I killed Finn because I was scared of what he would say about me. I was worried about what you would do if you knew what I really was. I never knew where I came from until we went to the priory. Mum said she found me crawling from the dirt ... a demon with black eyes." Her throat bobbed, and tears gleamed in her eyes. "I thought if you knew the truth about me, perhaps you'd rip out my heart and throw me from the window. And now I think maybe I need to be stopped."

Horror shot through my nerves, and my entire body went still. Disoriented, I felt like the world was tilting beneath my feet. "Where did you get that idea from? That very *particular* image of having your heart ripped out of your chest? Being thrown out the window?" There was only one explanation.

"Lilith. The ghost you thought I made up—remember that one? The one you'd never believe was real. She told me you would rip my heart out and throw me out the window."

"She told you that, did she?" My chest ached, and I felt as if the room were dimming. "How is she still here?"

"It seems she lived on in the soil." Her mouth opened and closed, as if she were debating saying more.

I stared at her. "And she is trying to convince you that you are evil? And that I will kill you?"

"Something like that."

Of course she fucking would. If Lilith's evil presence still lingered on somehow after death—of *course* she would attempt to ruin my marriage. In my entire long existence, I had never met anyone more skilled at deception. "Whatever Lilith left of herself here, whatever magic she is employing from beyond the grave—she is trying to manipulate you. She's trying to ruin us, poisoning your mind with lies. You aren't a demon. I can see in your eyes that you're mortal. I can smell that you're mortal. I can feel your emotions. I don't care what your mother said. How do you know Lilith didn't get to her as well? Or that whatever she said was the ravings of a mad woman? I've met plenty of demons over the centuries, and you're nothing like them. You are mortal as sure as I am an angel."

I heard her exhale a long, slow breath. She was shaking so much I knew her fear was genuine. "Can a mortal turn into a demon?"

"No." I inhaled sharply. "At least, I've never known it to be possible."

For a moment, my gaze flicked to the symbol carved in the wall—that malign symbol of Lilith. The Harrower had been tormenting Lila, hadn't she? Mentally ... physically. Regret fractured me. "I should have believed you about the ghost. Whatever it is."

Lila stared at me, her dark eyes gleaming with tears. "I can read a bit better now. I read about the Harrower. I recognized her symbol, and I remembered seeing it here. She's been knocking seven bells out of me. She says you will rip out my heart and throw my carcass into the moat. She likes to give me a taste of what that will feel like, with leaves in my throat, murky water in my mouth. She doesn't feel I'm taking this particular threat seriously. If I turned into a demon, is that what you would do?"

Dread slid over me, and an unfamiliar feeling like my heart was twisting. I lowered my eyes, trying to understand what this terrible feeling was. Shame?

No. Guilt.

I'd *never* felt guilt like this, a type of guilt I couldn't escape. This was an entirely new and terrible feeling to me. I'd killed countless people in my time. I'd been crushed into dust, vaporized by demons in battle. I'd fallen from the heavens with my soul ripped out.

But this was a new, unfamiliar, terrible feeling spreading through my body. I wanted to go back in time and change what I'd said. I wanted to believe her about the ghost the first time and stop this all from happening.

"Lilith attacked you." I reached for the side of her face, but then my fingers closed, and I pulled my hand away again. Did I have the right to touch her? I'd kept her here against her will, in isolation. Poisoned her with the pomegranate. I'd left her at the mercy of that monster Lilith. And now, by the haunted look on her face, I could see the Harrower had truly tormented her. "I should have believed you. Because I left you to her manipulations, and she got in your head. She is convincing you that you are a demon, that I will hurt you. None of that is true."

Lila brushed a strand of hair out of her face. "Okay. Tell me why she lived here."

"I was engaged to her."

I heard her exhale sharply.

I glanced at the broken window, the thorny garden outside. A sharp ache wound through me, and my fists tightened. "I didn't love her. She was incapable of love, and in those days, marriages were how alliances were cemented. It was after my fall. We had been bitter enemies before my fall, but the marriage was supposed to stop the eternal wars between her kind and mine. But the night of our wedding, she drugged my tea. She sent a mortal woman to my room to try to seduce me. It didn't work, but I got the truth out of the mortal. After the seduction, she was supposed to kill me. Lilith wanted to take down the Fallen, one by one. She thought we were standing in the way of her slaughtering mortals."

Lila's lip curled. "After what the mortals did to her, I suppose she would have been obsessed with revenge."

"What?"

Her brow furrowed. "So you ripped out her heart, and threw her into the moat? She's still angry about that. Very angry."

A sharp tendril of dread twisted through me when I thought of her. "She had a plan to raise an entire legion of demons from the earth. She wanted to kill each one of us and take over all of Albia, then beyond. She yearned to become a supreme Empress. She wanted to be worshiped, because when you have no soul, you have to fill the emptiness somehow."

The cold wind played with Lila's hair. She shivered and wrapped her arms around herself again.

I needed her to understand what Lilith was, that if her spirit lingered here, it was malign. That everything she said, everything she did was a lie. "She had to die for mortals to live. Someone has to do the dark and brutal work. And that person is me. That's why I was created. So when I realized that Lilith had to be destroyed in order to keep the world safe, I broke her ribs and ripped out her heart. I threw her dying body into the moat. I did what I had to do. And if I had not, she would have slaughtered every last mortal on earth who refused to worship her as a god."

A line formed between her eyebrows, and her eyes looked glazed. "She wanted me to know what it felt like."

"I should have listened to you."

"So you killed your last wife. You didn't mention that when you proposed. She kept trying to warn me." She glanced at the wall where I'd hung the drying flowers. "Now that we're getting to know each other better, care to explain why you kept the boutonnieres?"

I didn't entirely know. I thought I'd kept them because

they reminded me of Lila—how kind she had been to that little barefoot wretch, and how she must have been as a girl, barefoot and dirty and trying to scrape together pennies to eat. She was my emissary to the fragile, mortal world.

I'd never before given a single flying fuck about what it must be like for mortals living in the slums. It was my job to kill the wicked, not to feed the hungry. But now, it had started to take root in my mind.

And yet all those words seemed to catch in my throat. Perhaps because it wasn't in my nature to care for mortals like that. I felt cleaved in two once again—but this time, it was a choice I had to make. Did I believe Lila's warnings that she could be dangerous? Or did I believe my own instincts—that her heart, her soul were good beneath the rough exterior?

I plucked one of the boutonnieres from the wall. I twirled it between my fingertips and said, "I thought I could improve it."

"You fixed up the boutonnieres because you thought you could do a better job than a child?" She took it from my hand. "Why do I feel like you're not telling me the whole truth?"

My smile fell. "I could ask the same question, really. Why are you so convinced you are a demon just because a malicious spirit said you were?"

She held the boutonniere up to the light. "It wasn't just the ghost. Mum said the same. And because I met the spirit of the Raven King. He confirmed it."

I stared at her, my mind roiling like a storm. "Every one of these things could be a trick. Tonight, you will sleep in my room. I'm not going to let her torment you further."

Lila took a step closer, peering up at me. "When the Free Men raise the Harrower from the dead, will you kill her immediately?"

Shadows gathered in the corners of the room, darkness falling. My entire body felt cold. "Whatever happens, the

Free Men will not bring her back unless they have a way to control her. I will do what I must to keep the city safe." But with a growing sense of dread I knew that if somehow this turned out to be true—if Lila were going to turn into something dangerous—I would turn my back on my duty.

It hit me like a fist to my throat: I needed her now. I was tied to her.

Contrary to what I'd just said out loud, I would keep her safe first. I would protect her before I protected others. I would let the world around me burn to keep her from harm. Because she mattered more than everyone else.

That was not how I was created. And yet here I was—falling all over again, losing myself. I knew how dangerous this was, and yet I couldn't stop it. I was hers, and she was mine, and I had no choice in the matter.

Lila bit her lip, looking out the window. "Let's just hope this marriage goes better than the last time."

28
LILA

I sat on the edge of the bed in Samael's room. This room was much smaller than his grandiose library room in Castle Hades. It was circular, with bookshelves curving around most of the walls. There were hardly any decorations in here, just a few stark, silky banners, embroidered with silver Angelic writing and symbols. Even the spines of the books seemed to lack color.

A curving set of diamond-pane windows overlooked the moat, and the rambling ruins of an ancient church beyond that. Thorny vines grew over the stone walls, all the plants dead. Lilith would want to bring this place alive again. I guess I did, too.

Ludd sat on the windowsill, a little calmer now.

Nervously, I touched the acorn at my neck. I winced as I brushed my throat, where the bruises were still raw. Every time I swallowed, I grimaced at the fresh pain. If I was Lilith, how did she kick the shit out of me? I still didn't understand. Her spirit should be in me, not lunging out of mirrors to batter me half to death.

RAPTURE

I rose from the bed, inspecting more of Samael's room. To my left, there was a door, and when I opened it, I found a small stone bathroom with a copper tub and a narrow mullioned window. Dusky light spilled over the simple room. I crossed back into the bedroom, trying to fight the feeling of panic still buzzing through me.

I didn't want it to be true. I didn't want to be Lilith.

A four-poster bed stood against one wall. There was nowhere else for me to sleep—not a sofa or armchair. Seemed we'd be sharing a bed.

All this to keep me safe from ... the ghost of myself. My mind was turning in knots trying to understand it all.

In a former life, Samael had quite literally ripped out my heart. I had been in love with the Raven King. I had come back mortal, but I would soon turn into a demon again. Would I become Lilith completely—a new person?

I stood by the curving window, peering down at the murky moat beneath me. I touched my chest. It felt hard to breathe. No matter what, it very much seemed like I was going to die. Either Samael would kill me, or I'd turn into a broken monster.

I needed to tell Samael the rest. It wasn't just that I was a demon. I was Lilith herself. I was scared of how he might react, but he needed to understand it.

If I could truly be used as a dangerous weapon, one who would bring hell on earth, I *should* be locked up.

As darkness gathered in the sky, I realized I'd been standing at the window for ages, going numb. When was Samael coming back? And what was he doing?

I turned back to the bed. It smelled of Samael. I lay flat on my back, and closed my eyes.

As soon as I did, I heard her voice whispering in my mind. *You must be ready to kill him, Lila. You must find a way to get the upper hand. Seduce him now, Lila, and kill him, because he will show no mercy. You're still mortal. You can still kill him.*

"Shut up," I snarled, touching the acorn at my neck.

I rose from the bed and crossed back into the bathroom. I turned on the water, and steam rose into the air, clouding the window. I touched my throat again.

I supposed it made me a little more sympathetic when I knew what humans had done to her. To the old me. I could only thank God I didn't have her memories.

As the bath filled, I lowered myself into the hot water, letting it soothe my tense muscles. I grabbed the soap, running it over my skin. It smelled of rosemary, soothing. The dying sunlight angled into the room, glinting over the bathwater with orange hues.

Determination began to bloom in me. There had to be an answer. I'd always found a way out of things, hadn't I?

"Liiiiiila...." Lilith's singsong voice rang through the stones, and my breath caught. *"Lila, dear, don't you want to see what's in store for you?"*

I touched the acorn at my neck. I guessed it wasn't working that well anymore.

When she appeared before me, the air went out of my lungs. This time, she looked beautiful. Her hair was auburn, her eyes black as night. Her high cheekbones and lips shimmered with gold, and bracelets of the same color encircled her wrists, glittering in the dim light. She was taller than me, powerful. She wore a long white gown, like a bride, with red flowers threaded into her hair.

I hugged my knees close to my chest. "Lilith. We must stop meeting like this."

She smiled at me. "Do you want to see what he's going to do to you?"

"I'll tell you what I want to know. Is it true that I'm you reincarnated?"

She nodded. "Yes, and that's why I want to keep you safe."

I arched an eyebrow. "It really hasn't felt that way."

Her hair began to wave around her head once more, like she was underwater. "He's your enemy, whether you like it or not. You need to feel that viscerally."

I slid down deeper into the bath. "And how do I know you're not lying?

Her eyes were growing sunken, skin gray. "Some knowledge comes from books. Other knowledge comes from within."

"No," I shot back.

Her lip curled. "That magic you used, summoning trees and plants? That is Lilith's magic. My magic."

When I closed my eyes, I could remember exactly how it had felt to fall from that window—and the flicker of betrayal that had burned in me. Somewhere, buried under layers of ice, my emotions had been alive.

I opened my eyes, and my heart raced at the sight of blood dripping down the front of her gown from a gaping cavity in her chest.

Her expression was anguished, panicked. She stood with hunched shoulders. "Don't look away from me. This is your future, too, if you don't grow a spine. When my spirit comes alive in you again, Samael will kill you. Just like he killed me. You have the chance to stop him first."

I felt as if the bathwater had turned murky and cold, even though steam still rose from it.

"Come with me." Her voice rang in my head, and I felt it down to my marrow. She was me—powerful and terrifying. The source of my magic. The reason I could call plants from the ground to murder people. She was the reason I was so connected to the Raven King. Finn had been willing to kill me before. I wonder at what point they learned the truth—who I really was.

As if in a dream, I found myself rising from the tub, icy water dripping down my body.

In a trance, I followed her into the bedroom. And there before me, I saw a vision of Samael, towering over me. His wings were spread out behind him, and fiery chains wrapped around his powerful body. Golden whorls slid over his cheeks, and he was reaching for my chest—

The sound of an opening door made the image disappear again.

Now, the real Samael was standing before me. He wasn't wearing his cloak, just form-fitting black clothes. He'd gone eerily still, like an animal about to pounce, eyes like shards of ice as he stared at me.

My blood was still roaring in my ears, heart still pounding.

Samael's gaze slowly swept down my body. And it was only when I looked down at myself that I realized I was stark naked, a small pool of bathwater at my feet. I jumped backward and grabbed a curtain to pull over myself. "I thought you were going to keep me company so the ghost didn't return."

Samael remained frozen in place, flames flickering in his eyes. "Did she return?"

"That is why I'm standing here naked."

He arched an eyebrow.

I didn't want to keep this secret anymore. Mum was right. Secrets buried you alive, and I was suffocating under the strain.

"Lilith seems to think you will end up killing me. And if what she says is true, maybe I need to be ..." I trailed off. I couldn't bring myself to finish the thought. "I need a way out of what's going to happen. I might need you to stop me from what I'll do."

At last, he moved, prowling closer to me. "I told you. She's messing with your head. That's what she does. You thought Finn was manipulative? Finn had nothing on Lilith. He was an idiot nephilim. She's an ancient master of deception. Whatever she told you is probably a lie."

I cleared my throat. "She thinks I'm going to become a demon. I was born a mortal, but the Free Men will summon me to kill. I don't want to do that, Samael. I don't want to be a monster. Do you understand? Of course I don't want you to kill me. But maybe you have to stop me."

He stood over me, a line between his eyebrows. "What are you talking about?"

"You might have to chain me down if I turn evil. I'm warning you now. And I'm telling you I would rather die than be used as an instrument of the Free Men."

He frowned. "You won't turn evil. I am telling you that Lilith is trying to poison your thoughts."

"You told me," I said, "that you're the person who does the brutal work. Have you ever heard of a demon being reincarnated? I might be the reincarnation of Lilith. Born mortal, but her memories and power will be summoned again."

I took a deep breath. Maybe I should tell my secrets more often. Just getting this out felt like an enormous weight off my chest. I guess I had faith in Samael to do the right thing.

He went very still for so long it unnerved me. His gaze slanted out the window, dusky light shining in his eyes. "Perhaps it's possible. But I think whatever Lilith has said, you should assume it's a lie. I'm just going to hazard a guess that she wants you to seduce me and kill me. And it hasn't occurred to you that maybe she's using you to get revenge on me?"

I stared at him for a long time, clutching the curtain hard, knuckles white. What was the truth here? Lilith had wanted me to seduce him and kill him. "She's convincing. It's all very dramatic. There is a lot of blood and water and theatrics."

His features softened. "I have no doubt. But if she had a

soul, and that soul were inside you, she wouldn't be appearing as a ghost, would she? Her soul would inhabit you."

My grip loosed on the curtain. "Well, I did wonder about that. I'm just not certain of anything."

"I will assign some of my most discreet spies to research demon reincarnation, if you like."

I swallowed hard, hoping more than anything that he was right. "I think it's a good idea. And maybe we should wait on the wedding until you know whether or not I'm going to turn into a monster. I mean, you don't know for sure."

He studied me carefully, his pale eyes gleaming with a divine innocence. "No. I don't think I want to wait. In fact, maybe this will help prove to you how little mind I'm paying to the cautionary words of Lilith's ghost: I think we should marry tomorrow night. If you will accept someone mediocre."

At least he had faith in me. "If you'll accept any old mortal like me. And as soon as we marry, you become king," I said. "A leader of the Fallen."

He went quiet for so long I was wondering if I'd said something wrong.

His gaze searched mine. "Out of the two of us, I think if someone were going to turn evil, it would most likely be me."

"The reaper?"

"I have been enjoying killing far too much." His low voice sounded as if it echoed from darkness. "The Fallen are shadows of our former selves. Once, we knew right from wrong like it was the difference between day and night. Now everything is dusky and muddled. I question myself, always."

"Have you actually killed anyone who didn't deserve it? Anyone who wasn't allied with the Free Men?"

"I don't think so. Not in a long time."

I reached out, touching the side of his face. "You're terrifying, but I know that underneath you are trying to do the right thing. I think you're selfless in your own way. You took an arrow for me. You are committed to keeping Dovren safe. The Free Men are truly evil. Maybe it takes someone with a dark side to fight them. I think things will get messy. Blood will flow, but I know you have a good soul."

A smile ghosted over his lips. "The same is true for you. And that's why I'm not worried about you turning into Lilith." He frowned at the bruises on my throat. "Maybe I can heal that." He leaned down and pressed his forehead against mine, then cupped the side of my throat.

He closed his eyes and began to whisper in his strange Angelic language. The language itself had a power to it, each word vibrating through the air, skimming over my bare skin, under the curtain I was holding in front of me. I breathed in deeply. The healing felt warm, fiery. And as he spoke, the magic started to pulse into the skin at my throat, moving down into my chest. It was as delicious and addictive as he was, and it made me want to kiss him again.

As my throat healed, some of the panic began to leave my mind also.

Samael had to be right. Of course Lilith would try to manipulate me—it didn't mean it was true.

He stepped away from me again, his gaze still searing me.

"If we're sharing a room and I show off my *wares*, will it distract you?" I let the curtain drop just a little.

A muscle tightened in his jaw as his gaze brushed over me. I looked down at his hands, watching his fists clench.

He muttered something that sounded like "God help me" and turned away from me again. "Please put some clothes on. I'm going to start making preparations for the wedding. I will send Oswald up, and a guard to the door while I'm out to make sure you're safe." He shot one last look at me before he left.

I touched my throat where he'd healed me, still feeling the warmth that had beamed from his touch.

I was starting to feel like we were made for each other. And if he had faith in me, I'd have faith, too.

I wanted more of him.

29

LILA

Oswald laid three wedding dresses out on Samael's bed—one white, one cream, and one forest green. Already, wedding plans were charging full speed ahead.

He handed me a champagne flute, and I took a sip, staring at the gowns. I was already wearing a silky white bathrobe, belted at the waist, that looked good enough to be a wedding gown, as far as I was concerned. But the dresses were divine. Mesmerizing.

"Which one do you like best?" he asked. "We will have it properly fitted tomorrow."

I stared at them. They were all so beautiful it was hard to choose, with delicate chiffon fabric and stitching that looked like twisting, thorny vines over delicate bodices. "How did you get these together so quickly?" I asked. "Samael just decided fifteen minutes ago that we'd be married tomorrow, and now we have a selection of dresses."

"The count had someone buy these weeks ago. Seems it was on his mind." He took a sip of his champagne. "Do you know? He might be a closet romantic under all the brooding and killing. He's been making *floral* arrangements." He quirked an eyebrow. "If you ever see anything like that happening to me, please put me out of my misery."

"You'd rather die than arrange flowers?"

He adjusted his suit jacket and sniffed. "My manliness depends on it. There are certain rules to manliness, you see."

The corner of my lips twitched in a smile. "Interesting. Is there a guidebook?"

"Unwritten rules I'm afraid."

"And despite being thousands of years old, forged for divine vengeance and immortal, Samael's manliness is in danger because he did something with flowers."

He shot me a grave expression. "Absolutely. But don't you dare tell him I said so."

I sipped my champagne, the bubbles starting to go to my head. "And if it doesn't impugn your manliness to answer this question, which do you think is the best one?"

"I am far too manly to have an opinion on dresses." He blew a dark curl out of his eyes. "But a less manly person might suggest the white would complement your skin nicely, and it is traditional for brides, I believe."

An image flitted through my mind—a white dress with blood dripping down the front. Shivering, I shook myself to purge it. I didn't want to look anything like Lilith. "I think the green. It was the color for wedding gowns a thousand years ago, I think. It's beautiful."

He flashed me a lopsided smile. "Did you ask my opinion simply so you could disregard it?"

"It helped clarify my thoughts." I bit my lip. "I don't suppose we could send someone to commission a crown of flowers? There's a girl who sells boutonnieres under the bridge by Ducking Witch Park. She could make a flower crown."

"A girl? We could have a skilled florist do it." His smile turned wry. "Or Samael."

"The girl is very good," I said. "Her name is Hannah."

"I'll see what I can do." He took a long drink of his champagne, nearly draining his glass. Then caught my eye, his features tight, eyes narrow. "Sorry. I'm a bit nervous about all this. There is a lot to arrange. More advanced warning would have helped. We're supposed to set up seating in the ruined church, and I need musicians." He poured himself another glass. "That's not even mentioning the coronation afterward. Does he think I'm a miracle worker?"

"Okay, look, you don't need to babysit me here. There is a guard outside the door. And I've got my acorn. I will scream for help if I need it." I let out a long sigh, wondering exactly how long I'd need this sort of guarding. When Samael killed Lilith, would it all be over?

His pinched expression relaxed. "You're sure you're okay here?"

"Yes, go on."

I felt exhausted, and as soon as he crossed out of the room, I flopped back flat on the bed, arms outstretched in my silky bathrobe.

I felt a million times lighter since I'd told Samael my secret. I needed to do this more often. From now on, I'd tell the complete truth about everything.

I slung an arm over my eyes. I'd never spent a ton of time dreaming of a wedding. Women in my position didn't have beautiful weddings in silk dresses in ancient cathedrals. But I had imagined it once or twice. Vaguely, I'd thought I'd have a party in a pub, with friends bustling around. Zahra would be there, of course. Maybe the music hall if I married a musician. If my life had remained normal, maybe I would have found someone mortal.

With a sharp pain in my chest, I remembered being a

teenager and thinking that one day, I might marry Finn. I'd imagined Mum and Alice would be around to fix my hair, fuss about my dress. Maybe we'd get a band to play, a little flat in the East End. I'd never believed a wedding would be the happiest day of your life—I'd seen too many abandoned women to believe in fairy tales. But I always thought I'd be around family.

My heart ached, and I took a deep breath in and out. I'd lost Alice for good now. But maybe after all this shit was settled with the Free Men, I could see Zahra again. And Mum. Loneliness still gnawed at me.

My stomach felt tight, twisted in knots. I wanted to feel at ease with Samael, but I was still hiding one last secret from him. I hadn't told him how much I wanted him, had I? My pride was stopping me from doing that. And secrets kept you apart from others, isolating you.

I peeked out to look at Ludd. He cocked his head, looking at me expectantly. "All right, Ludd. You want to know my secrets? I have many, many secrets."

He squawked.

"Well, I'm afraid I have to confess anyway. Let's begin. I used to wake up before Alice in the mornings, but I'd get bored with no one to talk to, so I'd just *very* gently elbow her in the ribs over and over until she was awake."

Squawk!

"Yes, I realize I'm evil. But I already feel better, and there's plenty more. I stole a fish pie from Smithner's Market once, and it wasn't even good. I got drunk at the Bibliotek once and threw up on someone's trumpet and blamed it on Annie Craven, who used to call me 'Runt.' Once, one of Ernald's dock thieves cornered me and groped me until I punched him in the jaw. I saw to it that the cops were around on one of his jobs. Never saw him again. I think they threw him in the Clink. I'm terrified of clowns. They meet at a church service once a year, and I accidentally wandered in—"

Squawk!

"Sorry, am I boring you? Okay, well I've got more interesting stuff. I may not have told Samael *everything*." I lowered my voice to a whisper. "I have had the filthiest dreams about Samael, every night since I've been locked up here."

Ludd, at last, fell silent.

I closed my eyes, sighing deeply. "I know it's not a real marriage, but the truth is that I'm addicted to being near him. I crave his touch and his kiss. He is quite literally the most beautiful man I've ever seen. But if that weren't enough, he drives me insane with lust. That's the problem with touching an angel. Even one little brush with the feathers on their wings makes your heart race, and you need to feel it again. But it's not just that. It's the innocent look he has sometimes, like the world just baffles him."

I heard Ludd flutter away, and I peeked out from under my arm to see that I was alone. I'd managed to bore the crow.

I closed my eyes again, starting to become completely lost in my fantasy, even if Ludd was no longer listening. "When I'm around him, or even when I'm not around him, it makes it hard to think straight."

I could almost feel his magic moving over me now, snaking up my bare legs and under my robe. I felt my nipples going hard against the silk, and I lifted my knees to feel the cool air skimming over my legs.

"I dreamt he tied me up with ripped-up banners. I was face down on the bed, and he tied my hands right behind my back. And while I was completely vulnerable before him, under his complete control, he pulled down my underwear." I crossed my legs, my thighs clenching. "Then he sexually tormented me, driving me completely mad with desire. I was shaking, desperate for him to fuck me hard. I need him to just grab me and take me, and it's deeply inconvenient that he can't."

I stopped talking. That pulse of magic over my silky robe wasn't just my imagination, was it? It was real, hot, and powerful. Slowly, with a racing pulse, I slid my arm off my eyes.

My heart skipped a beat.

Samael was standing in the doorway, his eyes pure licks of flames in the darkness.

Listening to me.

30

LILA

My heart slammed against my ribs, and I sat up straight. I tugged the hem of my nightgown down to my thighs. "Were you spying on me?"

"I was, in fact, just standing in my room. You were detailing your fantasies for me."

My cheeks were burning, skin heating. "Exactly how much of that did you hear?"

"Since the bit about being addicted to me." He took a step closer. "And the dream about being tied up, face down. I find it very odd, considering you think I'm average."

Please kill me. "I was talking about someone else."

"Why are your cheeks so pink?"

I swallowed hard. "The champagne, of course."

A ghostly wind whipped through the room, snuffing out the candles. But moonlight still spilled over Samael. "Liar. I have ways of making you confess the truth, you know."

He moved for me so fast I could hardly track him, but in the next moment, he was kneeling before me on the bed. His hands skimmed up my thighs, and he slid between my legs, kneeling between them.

He leaned down, hands on either side of my hips. His dark, animal side was coming out, and it made my blood roar.

"You filthy little liar," he purred, his velvety tone sweeping over my body. "Are you ready to yield your sword?"

I took a deep breath. We were starting to play a very dangerous game, but I didn't want to stop. "And why don't you yield yours? You clearly care very much what I think of you, or you wouldn't be pressing this question. Why don't you admit that my opinion of you is important to you?"

"Hmmmm." His face was close to mine, and I stared into those fiery eyes, meeting their ferocity with my own. Fear fluttered through me, but the warmth of his sensual magic was overpowering it. His true face was rising, cheeks shining with gold swirls, but I kept staring anyway, holding his intense gaze.

He slid his hands up, gripping my wrists to pin me down to the mattress. "You still need to learn about honesty, I think." His dominating tone made my breath catch. He leaned down closer, his mouth next to my ear. "Just admit how much you want me."

Under the silk of my nightgown, my breasts peaked, aching for his touch. His powerful chest was hovering just over mine. This close, the full force of his magic was sizzling over my body, the intensity almost unbearable. I felt its electrifying heat washing over me, circling my thighs, skimming over my hips. An intense ache was building in me. I tightened my thighs around his hips.

His mouth hovered near my throat teasingly. "You were talking about me. And I don't believe that you think I'm mediocre. Might as well make it official."

If my arms hadn't been pinned above my head, I'd probably have reached up to pull him closer.

"Honestly, the needs of your ego are intense." My breath was catching, coming faster. He had me completely dominated, and I smiled, loving every dangerous second of it. "That word, *mediocre*, really got to you, didn't it? You can go ahead and admit that you care about my opinion, and therefore care about me. There's no shame in that. You don't think of me like any other mortal."

His mouth slanted over my throat, and his breath heated me. I wanted him to press his lips against my skin. Instead, he said, "I told you, I never yield my sword first."

He seared me with a dark, molten stare. An ache built between my thighs as the heat of his magic stroked me, licking between my thighs. My body was sensitive, every inch desperate for his touch.

"Your heart is racing wildly," he whispered. "Your pupils are dilated. You like the way I look."

"Fear response," I murmured.

For a moment, he looked completely lost—so much so that I regretted what I'd said.

I added, "Maybe."

Amusement danced in his fiery eyes. "I just want to remember what you said, specifically. Sexually tormented, right? Face down, I think, tied up, arse in the air. Quite the image, Lila."

I sucked in a sharp breath, cheeks burning.

He released my hands and pushed himself up, pulling off his shirt. I kept my eyes lowered from the intensity of his gaze as his primal side rose. So instead, I stared at the perfection of his powerful chest, sculpted by the hand of God. I wanted to run my hands over his chiseled abs, but it would feel like giving in.

"Hmm." I traced my fingertips over his abs. "Perfectly adequate. That should be enough for your ego, I think. Adequate."

Just as in my dream, he pulled two of the pillows into the center of the bed. A forbidden pleasure vibrated through my body as I anticipated his touch. Clearly, I needed to annoy him more often.

Slowly, his gaze swept over me, and he reached for the belt around my bathrobe. In one swift movement, he untied it and yanked it off. My robe fell open a little. I wasn't wearing anything underneath it except a pair of underwear.

"What do you think you're doing?" I asked. "Isn't this against your rules?"

"I'm an angel, not a saint," he murmured.

Samael was the last person in the world I should play games with—for his sake and for mine. But I felt like we were past a point of no return. I couldn't stop myself.

The bathrobe fell open, my nipples standing at attention in the cool air. My breasts ached for his touch.

Flames rose higher in his eyes, and every muscle in his chest went taut. He leaned down, hands on either side of my hips. Then, he lowered his mouth to my breast, kissing it lightly. *Too* lightly. He was teasing me on purpose, still trying to get me to admit how I felt about him.

"Reasonably average appearance," he murmured into my breast. "Passable."

The silky seduction in his voice nearly made me miss what he'd said. When I processed it, I frowned, gently shoving his shoulders away and narrowing my eyes at him. "Liar."

The corner of his lip twitched. "Is it just me, or do you care very much what I think, too?"

Yes. "No."

"I have ways of making you talk."

He pulled off my bathrobe—one shoulder at a time—and I felt goosebumps rise on my skin. A dark thrill rippled through me. I was sitting before the terrifying Angel of Death in nothing but my undies.

My heart pounded as he reached down for me and lifted

me by the waist. In one smooth motion, he positioned me face down, my hips over the pillows.

Oh, God, this wasn't another dream was it? I needed to *not* wake up from this one.

Gently, he pulled my wrists behind my back and tied them with the silk belt from the bathrobe. "Was this what happened in your dream about that *other* angel?"

"Very much like this, with that other angel, who definitely wasn't you."

But unlike in my dream, he immediately leaned down over me, the heat of his steely chest warming my back. He pulled my hair away from my nape and, resting on his forearms, grazed his teeth over my neck. It was a dominating, animal gesture, keeping me in my place, but it was also slow and gentle.

Pinned beneath him, I felt fiery pleasure coursing through my belly.

I craned my neck down, giving him more access. His lips pressed where his teeth had been, and his kiss sent more heat coursing through my body.

Ahh, the euphoric, ecstatic kiss of a fallen angel.

His sensual magic pulsed over me, like little phantom flames licking at my body, stroking between my legs. My body moved a little, back and forth, my breasts brushing against the sheets. I could feel every glorious inch of him as he leaned over me, pressing against me. I wanted him inside.

Everything, *everything* felt like a slow, erotic torture right now. His tongue on my throat, his chest against my back, the feel of his lips on me—all of it was a sinful pleasure that could rob me of sanity.

With his teeth at my throat, a primal gesture, I was his —all his.

As he pulled away from my neck, I turned my head to look into his fiery eyes. The sensible, controlled Samael wasn't there anymore. This primal version of Samael was pure fire, and a little rush of fear trembled through me. But then he closed his eyes, and his lips met mine.

He kissed me deeply, his mouth claiming me. The sweep of his tongue against mine made me moan into his mouth, aroused beyond measure. This wasn't like the torture in my dream. I felt something in his kiss—something more than lust.

He pulled away from the kiss again with a nip to my lower lip and sat up. Now I felt constrained. I wanted my hands free so I could run them all over him.

"Lila." His voice was husky as he threaded his fingers into my hair. "Are you ready to admit the truth?"

Desire was robbing my mind; I could hardly remember what he was talking about. "What truth?"

"You don't think I'm mediocre."

If I hadn't been so uncontrollably aroused, I would have burst out laughing at how much I'd gotten to him. Instead, my breath hitched as I said, "You first."

He let out a low growl, then pulled my underwear down.

With one hand gripping my hair, keeping me in place, he brushed his fingertips along the inside of my thigh, then slowly, slowly up higher. Oh, God, he needed to move higher.

I knew he could *see* exactly how turned on I was right now. Pretending I didn't find him wildly sexy was ridiculous. And yet, I'd committed to the game. I was going to see this through.

Just when he was about to touch me right where I needed it, his hand went still again. I could feel its warmth, just an inch from where I wanted it.

"Samael," I groaned. "Come on."

"Was there something you wanted to tell me?"

"You're nice looking," I breathed into the pillow.

Up and down, up and down he stroked inside my thigh, never quite reaching the apex ...

"Samael, come on," I whispered.

"Admit your dream wasn't about another angel."

I gritted my teeth, grunting, unable to focus on his words.

At last, his finger moved up, grazing so lightly between my thighs I nearly screamed. Slick with desire, I was on the verge of madness.

Then, his finger went completely still. I ached for more, for him to touch me harder. Tied up in the position I was in, I could hardly move—I could only buck my hips a little, trying to satiate myself against his hand. Even if I wouldn't say it out loud, my body was making it clear to him exactly how much I wanted him.

He took his hand away again, and I groaned.

"Tell me," he said.

As if from a distance, I heard myself whisper that I needed him. Somewhere under the haze of lust, I was vaguely aware that I was losing some sort of game, but I could no longer remember what the game was, or what the rules were. All I knew was that I needed him to fuck me *hard*.

"Whatever you want me to say ... I said it," I whispered. "Can you fuck me now?"

31

SAMAEL

Even though I'd known all along that she was lying, that there was no other angel she'd been dreaming of, some idiotic, primal part of me felt wild with jealousy anyway. I'd needed her to admit it. That was all I'd wanted at the start, or so I told myself.

But now, I could no longer control myself.

I wasn't sure if she'd said what I'd wanted her to say, but I could no longer remember what I'd wanted her to say anyway. There was a reason I should stop myself, but words were like smoke in my mind, flitting away. Meaningless. Only Lila had meaning, and the sounds of her excitement, the look of her perfect body—submissive and aroused before me.

When she looked over her shoulder at me, her dark eyes heavy-lidded, something in me snapped.

The taste of her lips had been intoxicating. I wanted her near me always.

I gripped her hips, pulling them up toward me.

Dimly, warning bells rang in my mind, telling me to stop. But they were quickly quieted again in the haze of desire.

The Fallen were slaves to lust, and I was no different. Not anymore. I needed her and only her.

Sliding in, I filled her, my mind going completely blank. She was perfect for me, made for me; I'd never experienced anything like this. As I moved behind her, the sounds of her pleasure brought me to an ecstasy I never knew I could feel. This was the beginning and the end. The reason why the Fallen risked everything, why so many had descended from the heavens. And I had never understood before why it was worth it, why civilizations would rise and fall for this pleasure.

I ripped the tie off her wrists.

This wasn't supposed to happen, but ...

She was moaning, shuddering beneath me, her cries growing louder.

Intense pleasure rushed through my body as relief gripped me at last.

I leaned over her while her body spasmed. Then, glowing, she rolled over and touched the side of my face.

I folded my arms around her, pulling her in close to my chest, and she breathed against me. Her body and muscles totally pliant and relaxed.

"Just so we're clear," I whispered into her hair, "you aren't just any woman strutting around half naked, and I wouldn't have risked my life for anyone but you."

"Just so we're clear," she said, "you are absolutely not mediocre, and I would never let anyone else tie me up like that."

She nestled into the crook of my neck, and her breathing started to slow. "You never told me what the ring says," she murmured. "Our engagement rings."

"They say *I am yours and you are mine.*"

"Perfect." She wrapped her legs around mine. "Why have you kept her room preserved all this time?"

"I needed a reminder of what would happen if I let my guard down for the wrong person. Luckily for me, you're not the wrong person."

My own breathing started to slow, and I drifted off into the deepest sleep of my long life.

I woke only when I felt a strange magic thrumming over my skin—a dark, invasive magic that should not be here. I glanced at Lila, sleeping beside me, the sheets curled up under her chin, hair falling in front of her face.

She was safe by my side, but unease built within me. In fact, it was rising to a sense of dread. I sat up straight in bed. Moonlight was spilling in through the windows, and the air felt strangely cold. My breath misted before my face. Rubbing my eyes, I felt a chill rush over me. Something was wrong ...

When I glanced at Lila again, my heart skipped a beat. The faintest wisps of magic glowed on her skin—pale silver symbols, slowly growing brighter. Sensing a threat, my hand shot out for the hilt of my sword, but it was nowhere near me. And what was I going to do with the sword anyway? Cut the magic off Lila?

As I stared at her, ice slid through my veins.

Was this another trick from Lilith's ghost?

Lila stirred, and when she turned to look at me, panic slammed into me. Her eyes were black as voids—demon black.

Not Lila anymore. I recognized her in those inky eyes—Lilith.

She shot up straight in bed. Her movements were completely different. My Lila was gone.

A monster sat in the bed beside me. My mind whirled, trying to make the calculations. I always knew exactly what to do, what my next move needed to be. And yet right now my thoughts were a blank canvas of horror.

As a demon, she could kill me now. I'd just turned myself temporarily mortal with what I'd done. And for the first time ever, I could be killed.

Naked and glaring at me, Lilith's hair floated around her head as though she were under water.

Had the Free Men done this with the Mysterium Liber? All along I'd thought they'd be raising her from the earth, not in a living person.

Where the fuck was my sword?

Her head turned—sharply. My stomach dropped with horror at the empty look in her eyes.

Lila. "What have you done with my Lila?" I stumbled back off the bed. I started stepping backward to the window.

"*Your* Lila? How sweet. But I am Lila. She's always been me, reincarnated. Maybe that's why you liked her." She smiled at me, cold and mocking. "Well, her memories are gone now. The Free Men helped me with that. And now I'm back. All my memories. Like that time you murdered me. Isn't it wonderful? I *did* try to tell you. You didn't believe me, my beloved. That's unfortunate for you, really. I don't think this will end well for you, my husband."

My thoughts churned like storm clouds. Hot violence coursed through my blood, an instinct to hurt her. To kill her. Even as a mortal, I'd be stronger than her. I could carve her heart out and throw her out the window a second time. But my heart was fracturing, because this was the one enemy I could never kill. "Is Lila still in there? Underneath Lilith, is she still there?"

She shrugged. "Who cares?"

Grief split me open. I needed this reversed. I needed Lila back—the one without the dark, twisted memories Lilith had.

I couldn't bring myself to kill her. Not if there was a chance I could get the real Lila back. Not if I could exorcise this demonic version of her.

Except she was going to try to kill me.

"What happened to Lila?" My voice boomed over the room.

She smiled at me. "She was just the sad, pathetic, mortal version of me. We have the same soul. I'm Lila with strength, power. I'm Lila with all the memories of every terrible thing the mortals did to me. Torturing me. Burning me. Over and over. That changed me. Lila didn't remember, but I do. And I'm not going to let you kill me again."

I knew I needed to act, but my brain was still struggling to keep up. For the first time in my life, I felt frozen with indecision. "How has this happened?"

She was still flashing me that horrific smile that made my blood run cold. "I was buried in Lila's consciousness. The Free Men found a way to summon me through magic. So, we made a bargain. They'd free me, and I'd kill some people for them."

"Kill some people."

"Mortals. Angels. I don't exactly like any of them anyway. Lila felt my magic all along, flowing under the city streets. Mine and the Raven King's. We created this city from dirt. And if she really needed it, Lila could use the power buried within her. Making plants grow, using them like weapons. That's my magic, my soul."

I recoiled from her, taking another step back. "You don't have a soul."

"That's where you're wrong," she shot back. "You were just too blind to realize. For centuries, my soul has been dreaming of the moment when I'd cut your heart out."

She lunged off the bed, snatching Lila's knife off the bedside table. It glinted in the silver light.

It could all be over so fast. I could snap her neck in an instant, have the knife in my hand. I could die, but I was as strong as ever. It would only take seconds.

It was, of course, what I had to do. For my own sake, for Dovren. I had to rip her heart out right now.

But I couldn't bring myself to move. She looked so much like Lila.

And maybe Lila was still in there ...

"I grew stronger under the ground," she whispered. "I got to know the dead, the discarded. The sinners outside the church cemeteries, outside the city walls. And now, I'm back."

I had to believe Lila was still in there. "Lila."

Her lip curled. "That's not my name anymore." I thought I saw a flicker of confusion in her eyes, but then they were dead again, black and cold as the night. "Don't worry, my love. They don't want you dead just yet. They plan to torture you first."

She moved around the bed, faster than I could have imagined possible, a blur of movement.

When she reached me, I grabbed her by the wrists. She fought against me, a million times stronger than Lila had been.

But could I end this?

My mind was a churning ocean of horror. Why the fuck hadn't I believed Lila when she told me?

It was only that she'd seemed *nothing* like Lilith. Nothing whatsoever. But I supposed memories, experiences, could change a person completely.

She was snarling and trying to stab me in the side, but I had a good grip on her wrists.

"Lila," I pleaded. I wanted her back.

Her dark eyes shone with rage. "Your mortal is gone," she hissed. "But clearly you love your women as weak as possible.

Submissive. I have a vague and disturbing memory of being tied up."

She broke free of my grip, and brought the knife down into my side.

Pain ripped through me, blinding. I'd never felt agony like this before. I'd never been mortal before, close to death.

As I stared down at the blood dripping from me, Lilith darted behind me and shoved me with such a powerful force that I felt myself falling forward, shattering the window.

Icy wind whipped over my lacerated skin. It took me a moment to register that I was about to die. As an eternal immortal, my survival instincts weren't what they should be.

I couldn't remember my fall from Heaven, but it must have been like this—that slowness, that feeling of being lost beyond all hope. The intense pain of being abandoned.

Vaguely, I was aware now that Lila—Lilith—must have missed any important organs. I wasn't dead, yet.

Primal dread hit me all at once—the hollowing of my chest that others felt when they saw my true face.

Glass had sliced through my skin. Under the night sky, I plummeted through the air. Time stretched out, and I dropped in slow motion. Blood streamed from the cuts, from the gash in my side.

We were supposed to be married tomorrow, but she was gone now. This was what it meant to fall: it meant losing your reason for existing.

The drop seemed eternal, all sense of fear dulled under cotton wool. My engagement ring glinted in the night, a little sliver of sunlight in the darkness.

As I fell closer to the moat, the certainty of death pierced me like a blade. This was the end of everything. Panic bloomed in my mind—the fear of things unfinished and questions unanswered.

At last, I slammed down hard into the murky moat, my

back arching with the pain, bones breaking with the force of the fall. Sharp cracks shot through my legs, my spine. Agony sank into my brain like thorns, robbing me of coherent thought. I thought I needed to swim to the surface, but my body was too broken to move properly. In the dark, I didn't know up from down.

Sinking, I drifted under the gloom. Dark water enveloped me, claiming me.

A flash of gold gleamed in the dark. Under the surface of the water, my ring glinted—a bright spark in the murk. I wanted to pull the cursed thing off, but that was a waste of energy.

This had happened before. This had *all* happened before.

Streaks of crimson mingled with the dark water.

I was still alive, and that meant I could still find a way out of this. Just as soon as I could figure out up from down, as soon as I could command my broken limbs to move again.

Air. Air.

My lungs were ready to explode. I couldn't breathe, and my throat was starting to spasm. Desperate, I tried to kick my shattered legs.

Could I drag myself, fingers clawing in the dirt, from the moat before I drowned? No matter what had happened in the past, I'd always found a way out.

At last, I realized silver rays of light were piercing the surface. That way was up. I could make it if I blocked out the pain in my body. Shockingly, I was still alive.

But as I swam higher, dread unfurled in my chest. From under the water, I caught a glimpse of pale blond hair over a black shirt. Alice stood above me, flanked by a line of the Free Men.

How had she managed to get here?

As soon as I came up for air, they'd drag me out. A world of pain awaited me.

But I couldn't stay under the surface any longer.

My lungs burned, and the need to breathe forced me up. As soon as my shoulders breached the surface, the Free Men lunged for me like wolves. Rough hands gripped my arms, dragging me out over the muddy bank of the moat.

I lay broken in the hands of the enemy.

It was Alice who'd done this—she'd escaped somehow, turned off the magical barriers from within. She had let the Free Men in.

All I knew now was that I would be tortured. And when they finished ripping me apart, they would kill me.

32

LILITH

Little pieces of glass glittered on the floor like jewels. I crossed to the window, shocked at the sharp feeling in the soles of my feet. Too sharp, strangely lacerating.

I wasn't used to feeling pain, and it disturbed me. Only partially conscious in Lila's mind, I hadn't felt a thing. Just flickers of awareness until the Free Men started summoning me through their magic.

Cold wind whipped in through the shattered window as I peered down to see Samael. The Free Men were dragging him out, just as they'd told me they would.

There it was ... the revenge I'd been craving. I wished he could have stayed in the moat longer. I'd been there for at least a day before someone dragged my bloated body out. The indignity of it had been horrifying.

I hadn't died right away. I had felt the leaves and cold water filling my throat, felt the emptiness of a heart ripped out. I supposed he didn't know that, nor had he thought about it at all after he killed me.

I cocked my head, staring at the woman with pale blond

hair. She seemed to loathe Samael as much as I did. She meant something to me, but I couldn't remember what.

I watched as she kicked Samael hard in the stomach. A hot, white light flickered in the darkness of my chest. Some part of me didn't like this.

That woman, that pale blond hair—

My fingers were curling into fists. Something felt wrong. I *felt*. That was wrong.

I gritted my teeth. I was getting confused.

This blond woman wasn't anything to do with me—not Lilith. She was a mortal from my phantom life. The sad, fragile life I was leaving behind. *Lila's* life.

I stared out the broken window, shocked by how much my body stung. The glass in my feet, the frigid wind bit at me.

I'd have to turn my feelings off again as soon as I could.

I was in control of this powerful body, and it felt good to be awake again. It was crystal clear now. My life with Bran, the Raven King, how we'd sailed together on the rivers out to sea. In the ancient days, the Albian clans had worshipped me as a goddess, building temples in my honor.

The bad memories were back, too—the years that had broken me, when *mortals* had ripped me apart piece by piece. Carving at my skin with seashells, drowning me, marveling that I couldn't die. *Witch, witch, witch*....

After I'd turned off my emotions, I ruled as Demon Queen, scourge of the angels. Until at last, I'd formed a truce and alliance with Samael. One that did not end well.

I shuddered, unwilling to dwell too deeply on those thoughts. I'd kill them all, and then I'd feel better.

But why didn't the victory of defeating Samael feel more thrilling? Maybe it was too easy? Hardly a battle. I had thought he'd put up more of a fight, but maybe he hadn't wanted to hurt the weak little mortal.

No, it wasn't just that. Something was wrong in my chest.

I felt too much.

I touched my heart. I could feel it beating as it should, a healthy rhythm.

Everything was working. Why did I feel like I was dying a little bit?

I shifted, peering over the shattered glass, and winced at the shards in my feet. The last time I was alive, I would have been able to walk over this without noticing. At least I healed quickly.

I stared out the window again. The Free Men were dragging Samael's body to a black carriage. Blood poured down his side and from cuts in his body. I wondered how many of his bones had been broken in the fall. Probably many of them, but I'd been careful not to cut through any organs. The Free Men wanted to drag out his death. Make a spectacle of it.

I clutched my chest again, finding it hard to breathe. What did I care what they did to Samael? Or the nephilim offspring.

Fuck the angels. Fuck their arrogant offspring. And the mortals could burn, too. I'd make this world a haven for demons alone, the children—the lost and rejected—that I'd raise from the ground.

Had the angels come for me when I'd been tortured over and over again until I lost my mind? No. I'd prayed and called to them, one supernatural to another. But why lift a finger for something that couldn't feel? That didn't have a soul? They were so sure on that point because they thought they knew everything.

Heaviness pressed down on my chest, so sharp I could hardly breathe. I felt like I'd been stabbed. What *was* that?

Something was wrong ...

I stared down at my bleeding feet. They couldn't heal as long as I kept stepping on the glass, I supposed.

I'd stopped feeling after the witch hunters broke me; I wasn't used to this. I didn't like this.

As I stared in wonder at my bleeding feet, a woman burst into the room. Tall and elegant, with a lace collar, dark skin, and a long dress that reached her ankles. I recognized her from flashes of Lila's memories, but I didn't remember her name.

She stared at me in horror. "What happened to Samael?"

"Oh." I shrugged. "I threw him out the window."

"What the fuck is happening?" she shrieked. "Why do you look like a demon?"

I cocked my head at her, then breathed in. I could smell the faint scent of poppies. Nephilim.

She had better hope the Free Men didn't find her.

I walked closer, glass piercing my feet. God *damn* it, why couldn't I turn my emotions off? If I couldn't change this, it was going to be dreadfully inconvenient.

"You're right. I am a demon. I'm not Lila anymore. I'm Lilith." I smiled. "I used to live in this castle, you know, in a bedroom with my symbol engraved in the wall. Some call me the Harrower. Some call me the Iron Queen. But once, I was Queen of Albia, by the Raven King's side." I raised my arms over my head and laughed. "The Harrowing Queen has returned. Let everyone know I am here to sow my army from the earth." I beamed, waiting to see her struck with awe.

But the woman still looked furious, completely lacking in awe. "You absolute twat. You're the ghost, aren't you? And now you're possessing Lila."

"There was no ghost," I snapped. "I am not possessing her."

My mind flashed with images of Lila struggling, under the illusion that a ghost was attacking. Lila's own buried memories had started to rise to the surface. My memories. They were more alive here, in my former home. She had begun to remember how I'd died last time, the memory of Samael murdering me.

All that fury had lain in a shallow grave in her mind, waiting to rise again. She hadn't known how to explain it to herself, had she? Her fragile mortal mind had turned the memories into a ghost. But it had been her own hands around her neck, squeezing, torturing. Battering herself. Trying to get the message through.

I sighed. It kind of put a damper on the glory of my return when no one knew what the fuck I was talking about. I wanted people to be awestruck, not baffled. Could I not get a moment of divinely inspired terror from this infuriating woman? All Samael had to do was make his eyes go a bit fiery and people fell to their knees. I needed something like that. A spectacle. Maybe writhing snakes instead of the fiery chains.

"The Harrowing Queen is awake now, at last. All will be well with the world again." I sighed. "I mean, not for most people, who will die. But for me."

"Are you kidding me?" she gasped.

I brushed a little broken glass dust off my arms. "Samael liked fragile, submissive things, didn't he? You seem the type. Unable to keep up with what I'm telling you. And Lila was perfect for him. Pliant. But she's gone now. And she deserved everything I did to her because she was weak."

What a nightmare the past twenty-five years had been with Lila in control. A world of darkness, quiet and muddled.

Only when the Free Men had begun to communicate with me had I started to come alive again.

They'd told me I needed to be ready for the Night of the Harrowing. It was my payment to them for summoning me. If I failed them, I wasn't quite sure what they'd do. I only knew they had powerful magic at their fingertips.

So far, I'd kept up my end of the bargain—delivering Samael to them. I hoped he thought of me as he lay dying.

Why was it so hard to breathe?

The nephilim woman took a step closer to me, anger burning in her eyes. To my shock, she slammed her fist hard into my cheek, and my neck snapped back.

She was bloody strong for a nephilim. The force of the blow shocked me a bit, and I staggered back over the broken glass. Pain confused me, distracted me. I couldn't focus on what I needed to do next, which was to kill her.

A second later, anger flared, and I lunged forward to return the punch, smashing her in the jaw. She stumbled back, but recovered fast.

In the next moment, she grabbed me by the throat and slammed me up against the wall. She head-butted me hard, and dizziness clouded my mind. If Samael had exhibited her level of viciousness, he might be alive right now.

Maybe my magic was strong, but the sensation of feeling had distracted me too much.

My head lolled for a moment, and when I could focus again, I heard her calling me *Lila*.

I tried to say *Lilith*, but with her crushing my voice box, I couldn't get the word out.

"I'm not talking to Lilith," the nephilim said, as if reading my mind. "I'm talking to Lila. The one with the soul."

She let her grip on my throat relax just enough for me to say, "I always had a soul."

But then she cut me off again, squeezing the life out of me.

33

LILITH

The pain made it hard to think straight. I was desperate to turn my emotions off, to be in control again.

"First thing you need to know is that I'm not submissive!" the nephilim shouted. "You got that fucking wrong. Second thing you need to know is that I'm not talking to you anymore. I'm talking to Lila. Lila, you do not have the same soul. A soul is made up of our memories, our experiences, a collection of flickering images in a flip book. If you have different experiences, you have different souls."

What the fuck was she on about?

"You have two streams of memories. Two life stories. That means you have *two souls*. And the soul I'm talking to is Lila's, because the other one is an absolute fucking arsehole. Lila, you need to gain control!"

I didn't like this at all. How did I block out the pain I felt? My lungs burned.

Kill or be killed. That was my motto.

I kicked the nephilim hard in the gut, and she flew backward, slamming into the opposite wall.

I doubled over, pain screaming through my throat. When I spoke, my voice came out scratchy and weak. "Oh, she's not getting control. Lila's not here anymore. She's weaker than I am." I touched my neck, wincing. "Though I'm obviously out of practice." I stumbled toward her, then grimaced. The glass again, cutting up my feet. "God damn it!"

The loathsome nephilim wasn't done. She grabbed a lantern off the dresser and threw it at me. I ducked, but it struck me in the shoulder. The oil spread over me, and flames and gas ignited on my skin.

Pain ripped my mind apart. I was burning; my back, my arms, my skin, eaten away by flames—

My mind snapped back to the witch hunters, and raw fear exploded in my brain. They'd found me outside the city, hung me from the city walls in chains. They had wanted everyone to see what happened to *witches*. I had been a goddess, once....

Panic erupted in my mind.

Burning.

A switch flipped in my brain, and I turned off my feelings at last.

Nothing. I felt nothing now. The sharpness in the soles of my feet was gone, as was the agony of my skin incinerating. By the smell of burning skin, I knew I was still on fire. But it didn't hurt, and I wouldn't die.

Only when the nephilim threw a blanket over me did the flames go out, but I no longer cared.

I tossed the blanket off, which probably would have hurt like hell if I could have felt it. I looked down at my skin, blistered all over but already healing.

"As I was saying," she snapped. "I'm talking to Lila. Because Lila—if it wasn't for you, I'd let this demon bitch burn. In particular, if it wasn't for Samael being deeply in love with you, I'd let her burn." She pointed at me. "Let me tell you something, Lila. Samael loves you, and I know you're in there. Do you know how much he loves you? He was out collecting acorns for you. The Angel of Death, rooting around in the dirt for bloody acorns to give you, every morning at dawn, because he thought they'd make you feel *safe*."

I wavered on my feet, trying to focus on her. For some reason, her insane rant had my attention. I stared, the icy wind toying with my hair. "He collected acorns," I repeated.

What did I care?

"Yes. And what else—he caught one moment of your conversation blathering on about fruit tarts with me and Oswald. Coffee with whiskey and cream, you said. Fruit tarts, you said. And suddenly he's putting pastries on your tray! He did it himself, arranging fruit tarts. Sending Oswald up with trays. The bloody Angel of Death. Arranging trays.

"Do you think the bloody Venom of God ever gave a fuck what kind of pastries people liked before? Do you think he paid attention to that?" she scoffed. "He did not. I can guarantee to you, Lila, he did not care one whit about anyone's preferences for baked goods. Until he met you, and suddenly he has these little things he cares about. These little details. So that's why I'm talking to you. I know you're in there. I know you're under the surface now, like Lilith used to be. There are two souls inside you, and if Lilith broke out from being buried in your mind, you can break out, too."

Slowly, a new, dull pain started to gnaw at my chest.

I shouldn't be able to feel anything now. But I *did*. It was muddied, hazy, but something felt wrong with my heart.

I stared at the nephilim, entranced by her. She had a power I envied, one I didn't understand. "Emma," I whispered.

Why did I remember her name? That was Lila's memory.

The Harrowing Queen did not need mortal thoughts distracting me.

She took a step closer, her eyes glinting. "Lila?"

My heart fluttered—pounding too fast. Was this fear?

I clutched my chest. "Something's ... wrong with my heart." The return of my consciousness to this body wasn't going as planned. I felt completely off kilter. Two seconds ago, I'd wanted to kill this woman as part of the glorious return of the Harrowing Queen. Now, I was telling her I felt a bit queasy, like a child looking to her mum for help.

I needed to get a grip.

Unbidden, an image flashed in my mind of Samael, hunting through the dirt for acorns. The vision seemed to steal my breath away, and I faltered, grabbing the bed post to steady myself.

Emma stood over me. "Your heart hurts, Lila, because it's breaking. Because you love Samael. And you know they're going to torture him. They're torturing him right now." Her eyes widened as she took in my naked body again. "Did you shag him?"

I leaned against the bed post. "You can blame Lila for his current state of mortality. That filthy little minx. Couldn't keep her hands off him even when they were tied." That had been one of the unfortunate moments my consciousness had risen to the surface. I shuddered.

"He's mortal now?" Emma shook her head. "The Free Men will kill him. And even if he does survive, he'll turn into the insane reaper. Where did they take him?"

"How should I know? I don't have anything to do with mortals and their psychotic ways." That was a lie. I knew exactly where they'd taken him, because I was going there next.

The Free Men had only agreed to summon me if I agreed

to help them. And they had enough magic at their fingertips that I didn't want to get on their bad side. Yet.

The wind whistled through the broken window, whipping at my hair. I looked down at my arms, watching the skin heal before my eyes. "See? No longer mortal. You may commence being awed."

Emma was still glaring at me. "Do you really think the Free Men intend to let demons live? The Free Men hate demons. They're not going to let you live when you've served your purpose. They'll find a way to end you. And all your little harvested demons will go with you."

She snatched another sheet off the bed and threw it on me. My nakedness seemed to irritate her, which only made me want to strut around naked even more. So I let the sheet fall.

I lunged forward and punched her hard enough in the chin that she flew backward. Her skull cracked on the dresser, the sound echoing through the room. She slid to the floor. Dead, I thought.

I dusted off my hands. "You've underestimated me, Emma."

A dull ache throbbed in my ribcage again. Frowning, I pressed on my chest. Under the numbness, I felt as if my heart were splitting in two.

If Lila was a separate soul, making me feel things I didn't want to feel, perhaps I'd have to exorcise her. I couldn't go around *feeling* things. Honestly.

I sighed, frowning a bit at the blood spilling out of the back of Emma's head. Someone would have to clean that up.

The Free Men wanted me to go to the telescope of fire—known to me as the Pillar of Fire. But before the Harrowing began, I really ought to put something on.

Flicking my hair behind my shoulder, I searched the room for something to wear. There wasn't much in here except a discarded bathrobe and a crumpled black dress at the foot of the bed.

Naked as the day I was born, I marched out of the room. The cool castle air chilled my skin as I walked. Once I raised my army of demons at the Pillar of Fire, I'd gladly kill Samael, if the Free Men hadn't done it already.

Then, the true Harrowing would begin. I'd harvest my demons from the earth. They would kill the nephilim and any mortals who got in our way.

As I walked through the halls, I peered out the windows. It was winter now, but even so, I could tell the gardens had gone untended. Now it was all thorny, dead brush, overgrown and uncared for. Snowflakes fell from the sky, sparkling in the moonlight.

I pressed my palms against the cold glass. As the magic crackled over my body, I called to the plants outside. I wanted them to live again. To bloom in the winter air.

Enough death. It was time for life again.

Magic thrummed up my feet and into my limbs. I stared outside as the dark briers began to bloom with red roses.

There we go. I'd bring beauty back to this place.

Smiling, I turned to walk down the hall again, but my chest ached. This persistent pain in my heart kept pulling me away from the victory of my return. I clenched my jaw, trying to ignore it.

I was in my old wing now, feeling at home among the tall windows, the high stone ceiling. At last, I reached my old room, the carvings on the door gloriously familiar. For a moment, I reached up and traced my fingertips over the carving of the raven and moon.

Then, I pushed through the door. The look of the place stunned me. Samael had left things exactly the way I'd left them. Which meant that my instincts were right, and I'd find some clothes here. Clothes fit for the Harrowing Queen.

I crossed to the wardrobe and flung the doors open. Rifling through the gowns, I selected a silky dress, midnight blue and flecked with little threads of silver, embroidered with crescent moons. Beautiful.

I slipped it over my naked body, and the silk rustled gently over my thighs, down to my ankles. It *did* feel good to be in a body again.

Then I turned, my gaze catching on a row of dried flowers on the wall, tied up in little silver ribbons. They were the only thing different about this place. What were they doing here?

Entranced, I crossed to them.

Without understanding why, I found myself plucking one of them off the wall. Dazed, I pinned it to my dress.

For some reason, the little dried weeds meant something to me.

34

LILITH

I looked up at the carving above the mirror and cocked my head. I could feel the Raven King's presence here. Vaguely, I was aware that he wasn't happy with me, but what was he going to do about that? He was dead.

I turned back to the wardrobe. Shoes would not go amiss. My feet were already healing, and I wouldn't feel the cold, but shoes would complete the ensemble. Little silver slip-on shoes. It truly was remarkable how Samael had kept everything here. It was almost like he had been waiting for me to return.

I looked down at the hem of my gown, twirling it back and forth, watching it swish. With my lovely new dress on, I marched through the palace. It felt empty in here.

Empty. My chest felt empty ... aching.

My fists clenched, and I walked through the bleak halls. Only the flowers outside were beautiful and lively.

When I'd lived here, there had been more servants bustling around. I'd kept them very busy.

I swept down the stairs. Already, I was imagining what it

would feel like when I summoned my army from the ground. All that buried magic, waiting to rise. I'd bring Albia to life again.

At the bottom of the stairs, I flung open the front door and stalked out, over the bridge that spanned the moat. Mist curled off the river, and a light rain was falling over me. A gauzy haze hung before the street lamps, and the gentle tap of my heels echoed off the cobblestones.

The Free Men were calling this the Night of the Harrowing. They believed that the Pillar of Fire was a good place to begin it all. Once, it was where a fire had ended. Today, it was where the purifying flames began. With my army of demons, they would burn and kill, and it would all start with Samael.

They wanted to make a spectacle of his death.

Things came full circle, didn't they? Once, he had ended my life, and now, I would end his.

As I walked, I touched the little cluster of dried flowers on my dress. A sharp pain lanced through my chest. In the dark night, I followed the winding streets toward the Pillar of Fire. I noticed some of the graffiti on the walls. *Albia Awake*.

I could feel my connection to the buried world of Dovren. Beneath the cobblestones, there was a world of power. The forgotten ones. The slaughtered. The abandoned. I could bring the dead back to life again.

I was ready to harvest the magic from under the city streets.

I lifted my arms above my head. "The Harrowing Queen has returned!" My voice echoed off the stone walls.

I still wanted crowds, though.

I'd get the crowds at the Pillar of Fire.

My thoughts kept going blank as I moved under the haze of numbness. It felt cold in my mind; the only thing distracting me was that painful fluttering in my chest. Images flitted through my head: a fruit tart; gray, innocent eyes that were trying to read me, shadowed under a hood.

At last, I got to one of the old, stony streets leading to the Pillar of Fire. Five ancient lanes converged where the monument stood. A gentle hill rose behind it to the rest of the city. The monument itself pierced the night sky.

Faintly, I could hear chanting coming from inside the column.

I approached and pulled open the door to the monument. There, I found Samael chained to the wall. Blood streamed down his chest.

A man stood before him holding a knife. And by his side, a woman with pale blond hair that hung like a lick of flame down her back. *Alice.*

"Lila," she said.

Anger erupted in my mind, and I found myself grabbing her by the throat and slamming her hard into the wall. "That is not my name," I hissed. "I'm Lilith now, but you can call me the Harrowing Queen." I let her drop to the stone floor and turned to look at the rest of their faces. There, at last, I saw the awe that I craved.

With a little smile, I turned to the stairwell that spiraled upward. "We made a deal, didn't we? You raised me, and you want me to harvest my army of the lost from the soil. Where is the Baron?"

"He's not here." Alice glared up at me. "I want you to know that the Free Men are legion, and we have the Mysterium Liber. We summoned you. We can gain control of the demons you raised."

"Is that a threat?"

She shut her mouth.

I glanced at Samael again, and he stared right back at me, his eyes gleaming with innocence. The piercing sharpness in my chest stole my breath.

"I'll kill him," I whispered. "In a few minutes."

His expression was so mournful—

My chest hurt so much, I nearly couldn't breathe. I stumbled, forcing myself toward the stairs.

I couldn't let his beauty distract me. But as I ascended, my mind kept filling with an unwelcome vision of Samael searching for acorns.

Why did this vision transfix me so? The acorns were something I hated. Lila had used them to shove me under the surface again when I started to rise. So why did I keep thinking of Samael finding them? That was something Lila cared about, not me. And she was interfering with me right now.

The fruit tart Emma had mentioned—the blueberries and raspberries had looked like little jewels, gleaming on top of the custard like it was a glorious crown.

I gritted my teeth, trying to force the image away.

I am yours and you are mine.

This was pure idiocy. I was here to begin the Harrowing, not to dwell on mortal trifles. Acorns and little gold rings ...

I found myself lifting my hand, staring at the ring on my finger.

"Stop it, Lilith," I muttered to myself, like a lunatic.

I shoved the thoughts from my mind as I reached the top of the pillar at last. Up here, there was a little balcony that overlooked the city, and I pushed out into the cold, windy night. The stone itself would conduct my magic through the earth. I wanted to see these narrow, winding streets fill with my children.

The frigid wind whipped over me as I stared out at Dovren—the winding river to the south, the rising city to the north, the jagged network of stone streets all around me. This city had grown from me, and I had grown from it.

I gripped the stone railing. Already, I could feel the city's buried power vibrating along the stones. Mortals were destructive creatures. They had slaughtered all the wolves, cut down all the trees. They had killed the elk and the deer. They had paved over the grasses and plants with their stones. I might be wicked, but I was a spirit of life. I would bring it back. I would make them rise again, more powerful than ever.

I had been living among the buried ones for five centuries. Now, my body vibrated with strength, and I could hear the song of their spirits starting to hum from beneath the ground.

As my magic worked, I watched thorny vines snaking up, wrapping around the monument. Red flowers bloomed from the ropes of plants.

The Free Men, dressed in black, had gone outside to the bottom of the monument. At last, I had the audience I wanted. What good was having magic if you couldn't strike fear into anyone?

A distant howling wound through the air. I knew they were coming for me—my lost children. In the shadows, glowing eyes prowled the crooked lanes. After all these years, the slaughtered wolves would find their home once more, here in the city of Dovren. The elk and the stags began to return, marching along the winding streets, their bodies smoking with dark magic.

Even as snow fell, flowering plants sprouted from between the cobblestones. Among the flowers, thorns grew—an army of their own at my command. The streets would teem with ancient life.

The Harrowing would begin.

Then, among all my marching children, mortals began creeping along the streets. They were dressed in black, holding torches. As they marched, they chanted, "Albia awake!"

I tightened my grip on the railing. I didn't like mortals among my army. Instead of the victory I craved, I felt mostly empty.

I turned back to the doorway and began to descend the stairs again. Now that I'd raised my army, I'd hunt down the angels first. Then the nephilim, then their mortal friends.

The death would start with Samael.

My mind flashed with an image of Samael drinking tea—

I didn't care what he loved. I'd bring the city to life once more. This city had been so quiet; now, I heard the faint music of life around me. *This* was true strength.

When I reached the base of the monument, I found it empty apart from a pool of blood on the floor.

Samael ... Where the fuck was he?

I rushed outside, and there before me, I saw my glorious army swarming the streets. But more importantly, Samael was here, arms still bound behind his back—just a few feet away from me. His head hung down, and two of the Free Men held him up. Ready for me to kill.

But first, I'd look at my crowd. Tonight, the shadows were alive. Packs of wolves and stags, plants growing all over the cobbles. Life was reclaiming its place once more in this city of stone. And although I loathed the mortals, I appreciated that they'd arrived to worship me.

I lifted my arms above my head and shouted, "The Harrowing Queen has returned!"

Now, at last, I had the roar of the crowd I craved. The Free Men were screaming for me, cheering.

"The Night of the Harrowing shall begin," I shouted. "It begins with the Angel of Death."

He stood shirtless, with his arms chained behind his back. I turned to him and stared at the blood streaming from his ribs, his shoulders—deep gashes carved into his skin.

I held out my hand to the Free Men, my eyes locked on Samael with morbid fascination. "Give me a knife, mortal."

Someone placed a smooth, wooden hilt in my hand.

I crossed to Samael and lifted his chin to stare into his eyes. That gray—that perfect cold gray pierced me to the core.

I couldn't breathe for some reason.

But I had to stay in control here. "You might think I didn't feel it when you carved out my heart, but I did. I felt the betrayal."

He narrowed his eyes, and I could see the flames smoldering there. "You tried to kill me, Lilith. You planned to exterminate all angels. I had a good reason to cut your heart out. I'd do it again. But I need Lila to live."

I frowned. "Maybe I had a good reason for wanting angels to die. And you were wrong. I've always had a soul. I had to bury it under the ice. But if you'd loved me enough, you would have brought it back to life again. You failed." I pressed the knife against his chest.

He really was shockingly beautiful, even if I loathed him. I pressed the blade into his skin, but my own heart felt as though it were being pierced by the same knife.

My hand started to shake. A sign of weakness.

I pulled the blade away from his chest and closed my eyes for a moment. My mind blossomed with an image of Samael, sitting down to arrange little dried flowers and wrapping them in silver ribbon. He'd made the flower arrangement I was wearing on my dress.

Confused, I touched the dried flowers. "Why is this important?" I asked. "Why do I keep thinking about this little flower arrangement?"

"Because it's important to Lila," he said. "Because they reminded me of her humanity. Because they made me want to be like her. Merciful. A caretaker."

Something was cracking inside me. "You collected acorns."

Alice stepped closer. "You must kill him for the Harrowing to begin. The Baron demands it. This is where it all begins. The cleansing flames. It is the deal the Baron made with you."

I turned and slapped her with the back of my hand, as hard as I could. She spun, falling to the ground. I felt something for her. A deep, fiery hatred. Were those Lila's emotions breaking through? "You don't command me, little girl. I might look like the woman who was once your sister, but I am not. You summoned me, but that does not mean you can control me."

From the ground, she flashed me a little smirk that made me want to crush her skull. "On the contrary ... do you really think we would have raised you if we couldn't control you? We gave your magic to you, and we can take it away again."

I didn't know if she was bluffing, but maybe it wasn't worth taking the chance. And after all, we had the same goal. It all started with Samael, right?

I turned back to him and readied my knife. The entire army of Free Men was watching me, torchlight dancing over their awestruck faces.

"The Venom of God dies tonight!" I shouted.

The Free Men chanted, "Albia awake!" The howls of my army filled the air among them. The wind whipped over me, and the city seemed to hold its breath.

A flicker of unease whispered through me when I looked into Samael's eyes again. Fire was rising in those innocent grey eyes.

But this was what I had come for. All that time, while my spirit slept in the soil, I'd longed for revenge.

He lifted his chin, staring into my eyes. Now, the flames

were intense, and his golden tattoos skimmed over his cheekbones.

"There you are," I said. "I see the real Samael is rising again. Maybe Lila had you digging for acorns. Maybe she thought that was the real you. But you're fooling yourselves. I know the real you. And the real you is pure death."

His eyes were shifting from that cold gray to bright flames, fury, vengeance, anger. How the hell had Lila managed to not run screaming from him? He was created for death, and he should terrify every mortal. Phantom chains appeared around his bare chest, blazing with flames. They started to move, snaking around him. Divine fire burned in his eyes, and he went still as a grave.

This was the true Samael—terror incarnate. Power like this was hard to look at head on, and around me, the mortals started to scream. I could smell the pungent stench of their fear.

But I wasn't like them, was I? It was hard to remember that when I was looking at Samael's true face.

I flashed him an uncertain smile, trying to hold his gaze, even if it was too much for me. Mortals, demons—we were never meant to see this. I'd faced him before in battle, and I'd defeated him. And yet he still struck terror deep into my bones. "I was wondering if the reaper would come out. You probably don't remember much before you fell, but I crushed you into dust once before. It will be nice to repeat that. But I want the reaper, and I don't think he's here. Not yet. I wanted to see him once more before I killed you. It was, after all, the reaper I first met all those years ago. But then you changed, didn't you? You became boring." I cleared my throat, trying to maintain control. Under the numbness, my heart fluttered, and I touched my chest. "You and I aren't all that different. If things get too much for you, if you can't handle what you're feeling, you will turn into the reaper. The reaper doesn't feel the pain in the same way anymore. That's all I did, Samael. I turned off the pain. I smothered it. We're creatures of instinct, aren't we? And that's an escape. You do the same thing that I do. You just never wanted to admit we were alike. But why not release yourself from the pain?"

"Where is Lila?" His voice was a frigid wind.

I shivered, trying to keep an easy smile on my face. "Lila. Always Lila. If I could feel anything, I might be jealous. Good thing she's gone now." Clenching my jaw, I stepped closer to him. His arms were bound by chains. He was mortal, and he couldn't hurt me. Breathing in his scent, I nestled in closer. He really did smell amazing. I kissed his throat and watched him shudder. I was in control here.

"Lila's gone. Dead, Samael. Maybe you'll see her in the afterlife. Wouldn't that be sweet?"

An intense pulse of power rippled off him, vibrating through my bones.

When I stepped back, I saw something change in his eyes completely—something I hadn't seen since the last time I defeated him—what he'd been like after his fall. It was that complete lack of mercy, a remorselessness. I'd broken Samael, and I wasn't sure he was ever coming back.

The reaper was here.

I knew better than anyone that once you turned things off, there was no going back. Why feel pain when you didn't have to? Why let yourself be tormented by feelings if you could go into a world without them? There was no heaven but glorious numbness.

I felt something again, looking at him. This time, it was fear gripping my heart. Even now, even under the numbness, he scared me a little.

I pressed the knife against his chest again, but one of Lila's memories started to take root in my mind: Samael was putting a blanket over the sloppy, slumped body of a drunk woman in a priory. He didn't want her to be cold.

My hand was trembling hard. Shaking so I couldn't hold the knife anymore. Bloody hell ... Lila was doing this, and she was stronger than I'd imagined. I was losing control now; my thoughts were flooded with an image of Samael kissing me ...

And then I felt her break through the ice, forcing me down beneath the surface again.

35

LILA

All at once, the emotions came roaring back into my body like a tsunami. The fear, the sadness—my heart breaking. Samael wouldn't last long unless I got him out of here. I had to get him to safety.

But it wasn't just emotions overwhelming me. My senses seemed sharper and brighter than ever, the moonlight like shards of silver streaming through the dark sky. I could hear every breath, every heartbeat of each living creature around me. Life seemed to have a seductive rhythm to it, pulsing through the air.

Focus, Lila.

What I did in the next few moments would determine everything.

My gaze flicked to Samael. He was near death, blood streaming down his naked body. An army of bloodthirsty mortal killers were waiting for me to finish him off. They were watching, eyes wide open. Just like they'd told me when they'd spoken to me through magic, they wanted to see his blood spill onto the pavement.

I had to get him out of here *now*. What if Lilith could take over again? What if she completed the job?

I gripped the knife, my mind roiling. Enemies surrounded me. All except Samael. But when I looked into his eyes, I felt my breath leaving my lungs. His expression was wrathful, merciless. The reaper.

I pulled my gaze away so I could think clearly. I needed everyone here to think I was on their side, that I was still Lilith. Numb and remorseless. I couldn't show even a hint of my real feelings.

"Lilith?" It was my sister's voice next to my ear.

My traitor of a sister. My fingers clenched into fists, and rage erupted in my chest. I wanted to turn and stab her in the shoulder with this knife, throw her down the cobbled hill. Too bad that would blow my cover.

I had to be Lilith now. Not to mention it would break Mum's heart again if I killed Alice.

So, I schooled my face into serenity, and flashed Alice my best lethal, Lilith smile. "I will kill him how I want."

I held out my hand and let the knife dramatically drop to the cobbles.

"I think you should know," she said sharply, "that we can control your demon army using the Mysterium Liber."

Shit.

There wasn't time to worry about that now. Only one thing mattered now, and that was making sure Samael lived. I'd take care of the Free Men after.

For what I planned to do next, I needed him to be unconscious. At the moment, he was rattling his chains, his muscles straining with the effort of breaking free. With the terrifying expression on his face, he looked like he was about to tear off his chains and start murdering everyone—including me. Samael, even in his mortal state, was the most terrifying thing around.

Act fast, Lila.

Time to draw on Lilith's powers. I crouched down to the stones and began to call forth the nightshade as the hidden music of the city hummed through my blood.

Down by the river, the Tower of Bones
If you're lost, Dovren is home
The lions are gone; the ravens are dead
The clouds up above, a storm ahead

The beautiful magic of the Raven King wrapped around me. From the snowy ground, leafy plants with purple flowers sprouted, winding into the air and blooming widely.

Deadly nightshade could knock a mortal man out. And Samael, for the moment, was mortal.

I closed my eyes, envisioning the flowers disintegrating and flowing toward him. When I opened my eyes again, I watched the purple flowers turn to dust. A floral mist whirled into the air before me, then swept around Samael's head. He breathed in the poison.

Alice coughed. "What are you doing? What is this?"

"Poison for my husband."

Slowly, his eyes began to drift closed. For just a moment, I saw a flash of recognition, like he saw the real me. "Lila," he murmured. Then, his eyes glazed over again.

My heart clenched.

I held my breath as he slumped to the stony ground. I stared for a moment at the pulse in his neck. I listened to the beating of his heart, hoping no one else was perceptive enough to realize he was still alive. I could now perceive things I hadn't before.

I wasn't mortal anymore. The Free Men had brought the demon alive in me.

"Is he dead yet?" Alice was asking. "Did the poison kill him?"

Her voice had always been high pitched, but it never used

to bother me. Now, it was like fingernails scraping the inside of my brain.

"Yes, he's dead. Now be quiet, mortal," I said in a low voice, a sharp edge in my tone. I could kill her so quickly ...

I felt no mercy for the sister I'd once loved.

I pivoted back to the waiting army. Outside, with the large space and the breeze whipping over us, I wasn't sure I could knock them all out quite as easily as I could someone standing before me. But I could try.

I shouted "The Harrowing begins tonight, and it begins here. Tonight, we purge our city of the scourge that has infested it. Tonight, I lead my army against that scourge. We fight together, and we cleanse this city!"

It was the sort of shit they would say—and I meant it. It was just that *they* were the scourge.

They raised their fists and torches, screaming "Albia awake!"

When I closed my eyes, I tuned into the earthy music of Lilith's magic swelling in the air, from the demonic army, from the plants. Power hummed over my arms, wrapping around me. I felt myself inextricably tied to these animals raised from the ground—the lost ones. They would do what I wanted. At least, until the Free Men took control. I just had to envision it.

I knelt down once more, connecting to the stones. In the recesses of my mind, I pictured the army of wolves and stags turning to attack the mortals. I imagined more nightshade rising from the cracks in the stones—my little army of weeds, blooming from the snow.

I could still hear the crowd chanting, "Albia awake!" They would get what they wanted—the streets flowing with blood—only it would be theirs.

Alice shouted, "What are you doing?"

She was the first to realize something here was amiss, while the others were still chanting, unaware.

I would do as much damage as I could before they got their hands on their pernicious book. I held my breath, hardly daring to move, and the world seemed to slow down. The true Harrowing was about to begin ...

The magic of the Raven King sang into my fingertips from the stones. From the depths of my memories, a word rose in my mind, one that meant war. *Rybel.*

Long buried, the word now knelled in my mind.

Rybel. I opened my eyes and exhaled into the frigid air. Time seemed to move so slowly, the snowflakes sparkling in the moonlight, my icy breath clouding around my head.

I rose and took a step forward. "Rybel!" With a flick of my wrists, I unleashed death.

The demonic stags turned on the mortals, goring them, antlers tearing at flesh. The wolves snarled, leaping for throats. My flowers bloomed, turning to a poisonous dust that floated on the wind. Chaos erupted, screams filling the air. The sharpest among them started to run, fleeing down the dark streets. Some used their torches, trying to keep the animals at bay. Others seemed stunned, still trying to take in what was happening.

From the corner of my eye, I saw blond hair streaming behind as my sister fled. Alice always knew when she needed to get out before anyone else did.

Stag antlers ripped through black shirts, through guts. Claret ran between the stones, little rivers of red. The air smelled of coppery blood, the sharp tang of mortal fear. I looked into the eyes of the mortals before me—some already dulling with the effects of the poison.

As I stared at the battle unfolding, pain shot down my back, like my shoulder blades were ripping open.

For a moment, I thought I'd been attacked, slashed from behind. But when I glanced over my shoulder, I found black feathered wings with veins of silver spread out behind me.

The mortals closest to me had drawn their swords, but the poison was already making them sluggish, confused. And I had the power of Lilith's magic now. Music floated around me, each living thing with its own tempo and its own vibrations. My body sang with dark magic.

I glanced at the vines surrounding the Pillar of Fire. My fingers twitched, and the vines snapped out from the monument, wrapping around the Free Men near me. One tendril at a time, the ropes of plants lifted them up by their necks.

A shiver of sinister pleasure rippled through me.

Once, I had thought the ghost in my room was a nightmare come to life. Turns out, I was the bloody nightmare.

My two girls, so different but so alike. One light, one dark. One good, and one evil.

And yet I would do whatever it took to protect those I loved.

I crouched down to Samael's unconscious body and lifted him into my arms. Even with my new strength, his enormous body was a strain. But I lifted him on shaking legs, holding him tight.

My wings began to pound the air—an ancient instinct that came to me as easy as breathing, now. Like my army of the dead raging in the streets, my buried powers were rising again.

As the night wind whipped at me, I took flight. Flying felt both strange and familiar at the same time. Dark magic slid through my veins, streamed through my wings. The icy winter wind rushed through my feathers.

Samael's dead weight was pulling me down, but I didn't have far to go. I just needed to get into the Iron Fortress, back to where the magical protections would keep us safe.

As I flew, I looked down at the sinuous city streets, where bright-eyed wolf creatures now prowled. The city looked more beautiful than ever. And when I looked to the east, I saw Clovian soldiers—a line of blue marching along the river from Castle Hades. An angel flew at the front of the army, his wings outstretched against the night sky.

Sourial.

Thank God Sourial was here to lead the Clovians, because it might not be long till the demonic wolves were working for the Free Men.

My memories of the last hour or so were hazy—pictures that guttered in my brain like a dying candle. I could see Emma's face in my mind. I knew she was angry with me, that she was stronger than I'd realized. She wasn't mortal. How Samael had ended up at the monument was a mystery.

Then, another image flickered in my mind, a faint flame. Someone falling ...

Horror struck me—it was Samael falling from the window. I'd pushed him and watched him fall. The memory pierced me like a blade to the heart.

I pulled him in closer, watching his chest rise and fall. Snowflakes dusted his dark eyebrows, his hair.

Lilith was powerful, but he was the Angel of Death. If he'd lost a fight to her, it must have been because he wasn't really trying. Had he been unwilling to hurt her if it meant hurting me?

When I thought of his face, before I'd poisoned him, the knife in my heart twisted further. That merciless look, like he no longer knew me. He'd been turning into the reaper. Would I get my Samael back?

And even if I could, would Lilith let me? I felt as if an axe were hanging above my head, waiting to drop. I couldn't imagine how furious Lilith must be to realize I gave her demon army over to the Free Men, just to save the life of a man she loathed more than anything.

Another image burst into my mind—Emma lying still on the floor of my room, like a corpse ...

I wanted to be sick.

At last, the castle came into view, and I angled my wings. I swooped down toward the gate, trying to coast over it. But as I got closer, pain shot through my body, and I nearly dropped Samael.

I tried to soar over the iron gate, but when I did, I felt my wings arcing, turning me back in the other direction. Searing magic burst and buzzed over my skin every time I got close.

It took me a few moments to understand this was the magical defense keeping me away. I had been able to get in on my own before.

But I wasn't just Lila anymore.

My arm muscles burned with the effort of carrying Samael. I was no longer welcome here.

So, I circled back around again, outside the castle gates, and touched down by the river walk. It wasn't even locked, just curling, spiked wrought iron that spread out in each direction, with jagged gaps and an open arch before me. But the magical wards would keep me from crossing through.

"Emma!" I screamed. "Oswald!"

In only took a few more moments for the door to slam open. Emma stood in the castle entrance, the wind toying with her hair. Her dress looked ragged, bloody. Part of me was relieved that Lilith hadn't killed her ...

The other part of me was honestly a little scared. The look on her face was murderous, and she was marching toward me with a knife in her hand.

"Emma," I shouted, "it's me, Lila!"

"Lila doesn't have wings!" she shouted back.

"It's me. You call yourself Seneschal and you want to

throw balls here and fall in love. It's me! I got control from Lilith. Let me in."

"I'm going to need more than that."

"We went through the books together, and you helped me read. You fancied one of the pictures of the demons with big horns and then felt bad about it."

"Okay," she said tentatively. "It's you." Her gaze lowered to Samael, horror creeping over her features. "Did you kill him? Is he dead?"

"No, he's just unconscious from nightshade. And there's a battle raging between demons and Free Men and the Clovian army."

She nodded. "Sourial showed up and roused me out of unconsciousness. I sent him there."

With a deep breath, she closed her eyes and began chanting in Angelic. I felt a magical electrical hiss pulse over my body, then she beckoned me through the gates.

As soon as I heaved Samael's enormous body through, his eyes snapped open, and he was on his feet again. Fire blazed in his eyes, golden tattoos gleaming on his cheekbones. Never before had I seen someone shift so fast from unconscious to ready for battle.

He went very still, cocking his head like a strange, primordial creature. I took a step back from him and felt my dark wings retract into my back again. *Ouch*.

Emma shifted in front of him, her hands out. "It's Lila. For now. We probably need to lock her up in case Lilith returns. Samael, I can't look at you. Does no one wear clothes anymore?"

I looked down at my hands. "She's right. I need to be locked up."

I glanced at Samael again. The moonlight sculpted his muscled body, and the wind rushed off the river, toying with his hair. Already, his wounds were healing, the blood no longer flowing. He hadn't moved at all—eerily still, eyes pure fire and locked on me.

"Samael?" Emma shielded her eyes. "Sourial needs you. By the monument."

"You saw the Free Men, right?" I asked him. "There were a few hundred? I know that's not all of them. Alice ran away. She said they might be able to control Lilith's demon army." I cleared my throat, and clenched my fists. "Sorry for, uh ... sorry for raising the demon army."

Darkness billowed around Samael, staining the air with ink. Instinctively, I took another step back from him. Even if I was back in my own body, I didn't think Samael quite was. Chains of fire writhed around him, and his dark wings spread out behind his back. The flames in his eyes looked like reflections from the depths of Hell.

At last, he spoke, and his voice tolled like a funeral bell. "We'll both need to be chained. I crave vengeance and blood."

Emma stared at him. "Okay, simmer down, reaper. You can get the vengeance and blood as soon as I get your sword and some clothes. Get some pants on for that, you know?" She whirled, heading back into the castle.

I needed to bring Samael back. And as I looked at him—his true face—I realized I was no longer scared of him. I didn't think this *was* the real Samael. The real Samael could love.

I closed the distance and pressed my palm against his cheek. "It's me. Lila." I wanted to tell him I was exactly the same as I was before, as I was earlier today, when he'd told me *I am yours and you are mine*. But the fact was that I wasn't.

Memories from a distant past flickered in the hollows of my skull. I felt her pain. "Lilith wants you to know that she did have a soul. And she felt it when you killed her. She didn't feel the pain. She felt betrayal."

For a moment, the flames in his gaze died down, and anguish replaced them. He covered my hand with his, and his eyes searched mine.

Then he shuddered and pulled my hand from his cheek. "We are dangerous for each other. We are destined to hurt each other. And you never had a choice, did you? You didn't have a choice about coming with me to Castle Hades; you thought I'd kill you. I could have found a mortal willing to marry me. But I trapped you, didn't I? I thought it had to be you. Of course you tried to kill me. Angel and mortal, or angel and demon—we are from different worlds, and we are destined to hurt each other. In each others' company, we are dangerous."

I felt a sort of panic rising, realizing how scared I was of losing him. "I wasn't trapped here. I chose to be here in the Iron Fortress. I could have left long ago."

His fingers twitched. "You were locked up here, unable to leave without feeling pain."

"No, I figured out the fruit was poisoned. The bright red one with all the seeds."

At last, he said, "Pomegranate. So why didn't you leave if you knew how?"

"Because I didn't want to. We're on the same team, even if we're different. And I don't want to leave now. I'm going to be here, chained up, when you get back." I winced. "Or Lilith will be here."

A frost chilled the air, and shadows pulsed around him. "Like I said. We're dangerous for each other. And I can feel the battle calling to me."

The door opened again, and Emma rushed out, carrying clothes for Samael, and his sword. He pivoted toward her, grabbing the sword and his cloak. He didn't seem to care about the rest of his clothes.

I watched him wrap the cloak around himself, feeling like

my heart was breaking. What if I wasn't here when he got back? What if it was Lilith?

Emma grabbed me, pulling me toward the door. "You need chains, while you're still compliant."

As we got to the door, I looked for Samael. But he'd already disappeared into the night.

THE CHAINS CLANKED AS I TRIED TO BRING MY GLASS OF wine to my lips. The metal chafed at my wrists, and I spilled a bit of claret on myself. "How exactly were you able to get these chains set up so quickly?" I asked.

"You don't want to know." Emma paced the room, glancing out the window. "Shouldn't they be back by now? I hope they kill every last one of them." She looked at me. "I need him back. And Sourial. Sourial is the most beautiful man I've ever laid eyes on, and I intend to make him my husband someday."

I glanced out the window at the night sky, wishing I could see Samael swooping back toward the castle. "I think they'll be okay. The Free Men were not in good shape when I left. I filled the air with nightshade." I took another sip of wine, trying to calm my nerves. "I think they're probably just hunting the people who tried to escape."

I wanted to go out there, wings and all, and get a bird's eye view of the situation. But roaming free was too much of a risk when I shared this body with Lilith.

What worried me, though, wasn't Samael's fate. What worried me more was what he'd said before he left, with such dark certainty. *We're dangerous for each other.*

I wanted to convince him that wasn't the case—that we could be stronger together.

The sound of footfalls outside the room had my heart

racing faster. I wanted to see Samael's face, and when the door swung open, my heart rate picked up speed.

But when I saw Sourial, my stomach sank.

I sat up straight, the chains pulling at my wrists. "What happened?"

He crossed into the room, and rubbed his eyes. Blood and dirt smudged his face.

"Where's Samael?" I asked.

He blinked, looking at me. "He has asked me to lock him in the dungeon of Castle Hades. It seems he didn't want to stop killing."

I inhaled sharply. "Wonderful. And the Free Men?"

"Some of them got away. Others were mauled by the animals. Our soldiers were affected by the poison in the air, but it didn't matter. There wasn't much of a fight left." His voice sounded weary, and he glanced at Emma. "We think most of the Free Men assembled there were lower ranks. Expendable to their leaders. We still have to hunt down the real threat."

"And the army of wolves?" I felt weirdly attached to them, a strange sense that we were from the same family.

"Gone," he said. "For now. We will be searching for them, and for the Free Men who escaped. And we need to make sure you stay exactly where you are, Lila. Nothing in this world is more dangerous right now than Lilith."

"We need to figure out how to get Lilith out of my body," I said. "Or I'll be living with a sword over my neck. And permanently chained to this bed." And unfortunately, it would not be in a fun way.

Sourial narrowed his eyes at me. "I'm not sure it will be that simple. She's part of you, isn't she? Maybe she's a dark side you need to control."

Emma fluttered her eyelashes at Sourial. "Well, we can try to get rid of Lilith. Lila is going to be Samael's wife." She frowned, looking at me out of the corner of her eye. "*Is* she still going to be his wife?"

Sourial's expression was sorrowful. "He needs to marry a mortal. Not a demon. They all remember what happened the last time he tried to marry a demon. And besides, they don't want him to be any more powerful than they are in case he goes mad with power. Only a mortal can achieve that balance."

My heart ached, and I felt like I couldn't breathe. "I'm right here," I muttered. "In case you forgot."

Sourial nodded at me. "Will those chains hold Lilith?"

Emma folded her arms, looking at me as she exhaled loudly. "Yes. And we will station guards to knock her out if necessary. They can watch over her at all times."

My throat tightened, and I felt more isolated than ever. What was my role here now? All this time, becoming Samael's wife had been my leverage. It was what kept me safe, protected. Now? I was just a liability. How long until they decided it was best to get rid of me?

"I'll return to Castle Hades," said Sourial, still ignoring me, looking at Emma. "I know Samael trusts you. So I trust that you won't tell anyone about his current situation."

"The reaper?" She nodded. "I won't say a word."

"He still plans to be King of the Fallen. He must be sane for that."

Without another word to me, Sourial slipped into the darkness of the hall.

Emma turned to me, her expression tight. I felt something change in the air. It wasn't clear what my purpose was here anymore.

"I can use the demon powers for good," I blurted. "If I can control Lilith. Samael controls his reaper, doesn't he? I mean, normally."

Her forehead wrinkled. "Perhaps. The guards will be here soon." She turned and crossed out of the room.

It was just me and these four walls again.

I swallowed hard, shocked at how much it hurt that Samael and I would no longer be together.

I glanced out the window at the dark night sky.

I wanted to see him more than anything. I needed to convince him that he was wrong—that more than being dangerous for each other, we needed each other. I was sure that I'd changed him, helped him let down his guard for a little while.

And if anyone understood how to manage a dark side, if anyone could help me get through this, it was him.

※

THANK YOU FOR READING *RAPTURE*.

Possessed will be the final book in the Hades Castle series.

You can preorder it now.

The release date will likely be moved to an earlier time so make sure to stay in touch!

To get a notification of the release date of Possessed, you can sign up to my newsletter, or join my facebook group, **C.N. Crawford's Coven.**

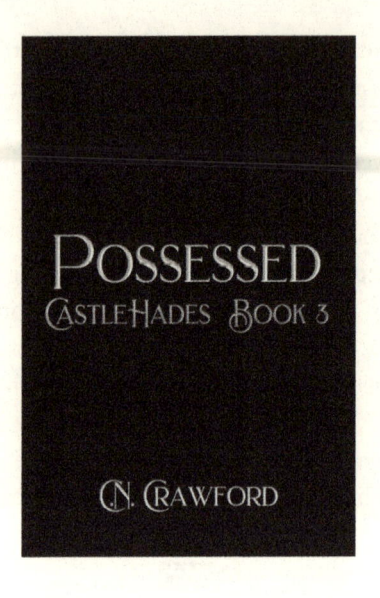

C.N. CRAWFORD

POSSESSED
CASTLE HADES BOOK 3

C.N. CRAWFORD

36

ALSO BY C.N. CRAWFORD

Follow us on Amazon and check out our page for a full list of our books
Follow us on Amazon

ACKNOWLEDGMENTS

Thanks to my supportive family, and to Michael Omer for his critiques and for being a cheerleader.

Isabella and Jen are my fabulous editors for this book. Thanks to my advanced reader team for their help, and to C.N. Crawford's Coven on Facebook!

Made in the USA
Las Vegas, NV
30 January 2022